*Real Mothers*

# Real Mothers

## SHORT STORIES BY AUDREY THOMAS

TALONBOOKS · VANCOUVER · 1981

copyright © 1981 Audrey Thomas

published with assistance from the Canada Council and the
Government of British Columbia through the British
Columbia Cultural Fund and the Western Canada Lottery
Foundation

*Talonbooks*
*201 1019 East Cordova*
*Vancouver*
*British Columbia V6A 1M8*
*Canada*

This book was typeset by Mary Schendlinger, designed
by David Robinson and printed in Canada by Hignell
for Talonbooks.

Second printing: April 1982
Third printing: December 1986

Some of these stories have appeared in: *The Capilano Review,*
*Chatelaine, Saturday Night* and *Toronto Life.* Both "Natural
History" and "Galatea" have been broadcast on CBC Radio's
*Anthology.*

Canadian Cataloguing in Publication Data

Thomas, Audrey, 1935-
　　Real mothers

ISBN 0-88922-191-X

I. Title.
PS8539.H64R4　　　C813'.54　　　C81-091330-5
PR9199.3.T49R4

*to my sister, Jean*

Contents

# REAL MOTHERS

After Marie-Anne's parents had been separated for about a year, her mother joined Weight Watchers, lost thirty pounds, and decided to go back to school. At first — for quite a long time really — Marie-Anne, and her older brother, Clayton, who was sixteen, and her little sister, Patty, were very pleased about all this. Their mother had been sad for months and months and Marie-Anne, who shared a large room in the basement with Patty, used to hate to hear the sound of her mother's weeping, which, through some trick of the hot air vents, came down to her, sometimes in the middle of the night, from the second-floor bedroom. She was sure that her mother thought that all the children were asleep (Clayton wouldn't have heard anyway, as he had a private suite of his own, on the other side of the basement) and she felt as if she were eavesdropping. She wanted to go up and comfort her mother. but didn't know what to say. She lay awake and tried to understand about her father having to leave. He had taken her on a long walk to Third Beach one day and explained that he and her mother no longer "related" to one another, and that, in the end, her mother would probably thank him. Marie-Anne couldn't follow all this, particularly the bit about thanking him. She wanted to tell him about the crying, but she knew that that would be a betrayal of her mother and it probably wouldn't do any good anyway. So, she simply kicked at the sand and said, "Can we go home now?" He suggested that they stop in at the Big Scoop on the way home, but she said that she wasn't hungry. She could tell from her father's face that he was disappointed in her, but she couldn't help it. Just before they got to the house, he said, "Maybe I'll bring Ardelle along next time; I'd really like you to get to know her."

"I already know her," Marie-Anne said. Ardelle had been one of her father's students and had come to parties and seminars at the house.

"I mean, *really* know her," her father said, putting his hand on her shoulder.

She had not replied; it was very hard to keep from crying, she loved him so much.

He stopped at the bottom step. "We spent seventeen years as vegetables, Marie-Anne. You've really got to try and understand!"

"I've got a lot of homework to do," she said and ran up the steps.

She had seen the back of her mother's head. She was sitting on the couch by the front window. Marie-Anne knew that he had seen her mother's head too.

His voice came after her, purposefully cheerful. "I'll call you next week."

Patty and her mother were carving a pumpkin. It all seemed staged somehow. Carving the Hallowe'en pumpkins was something that her father had always helped them with. Her mother had on the velour jersey that he had given her last Christmas. It was too tight now, but it brought out all the red highlights in her hair. Marie-Anne had seen her mother look to see if anyone else had come in. She must have known from the footsteps on the porch, but she couldn't help looking anyway. Marie-Anne felt helpless and angry, as if she had let her mother down. She had been supposed to entice him inside to see how well she was "coping." (It was one of her mother's new words; she used it a lot on the telephone to her friends: "Oh, we're coping, thanks." "Oh, I'm managing to cope with it all somehow.") Marie-Anne told the same plausible lie about the homework and hurried downstairs.

She had broken a piece of Waterford glass once, when she was younger. It had been in her father's family for ages. She looked and looked for all the pieces and tried to fit them together, but of course, it wouldn't work. Her face was so close to the kitchen floor that she pricked her nose on a splinter and she began to howl. Her father and mother rushed in and hugged her, and kissed her nose and laughed. They said that it didn't matter, it was an accident. It took her a long time to calm down. She was finally tucked in bed with a bowl of milk toast. Now, she lay on her bed, dry-eyed and desperate. It wasn't her fault; it wasn't anybody's fault. It was like an accident. She heard her mother often say, as though to get it through her head, "Oh, I'm separated." Marie-Anne had never heard of separated children — "Oh, I'm a separated child" — but she didn't see how she was going to be able to stand it. Clayton didn't seem to pay much attention to what was going on. He was into a lot of sports, and also, he had piles of homework, so they didn't see much of him; he was more like a long-standing boarder, these days, than her brother. He did his share of the chores and always made breakfast on Sundays, but most nights, he vanished to his suite, right after the washing-up. She knew that he had been to visit their father, but he never talked about it. One night, quite late, she heard him upstairs in the kitchen, shouting at their mother, who must have known or suspected where he had gone, must have waited up for him.

"I refuse to discuss him with you or you with him," he cried. "Jesus, will you leave me alone!"

Marie-Anne heard him slam the kitchen door and pound down the back steps, sobbing. It was the first time in years that she heard her brother cry, but strangely enough, she found his crying comforting, not frightening, for it proved that he cared. Patty slept through all the noise and Marie-Anne got up and went over to look at her. She tried to remember what it must have been like to be seven and a half years old. She shared this room with Clayton then, until the baby was out of her crib, and her brother was given a room upstairs. Had he ever come over and looked down at her sleeping? But it would have been

11

different; he would have been over ten. They were both still little kids and Patty was "the Baby." If Patty woke up early, Marie-Anne used to get her out of the crib and take her into bed. Clayton pretended that he didn't like the baby very much and he said to his friends that all she ever did was shit and pee; but in the early mornings, after Marie-Anne had changed her and cleaned her up, they would tickle her and make her laugh, examine her little hands and feet. Clayton once said that the soles of the baby's feet were the same colour as pencil erasers, the same dusty pink, and Marie-Anne thought that was terribly unromantic, but very true. Their father was English and still called many things by funny names. He called erasers "rubbers," for instance. So, Clayton and Marie-Anne began calling Patty, "Baby Rubber," and "Rubber Baby," and the baby just laughed and pulled at their hair. Sometimes, Clayton would put the baby, stomach-down, on top of his head and hold her there; she loved that. Pretty soon, their mother would stumble down in her old blue dressing gown, sit in the rocking chair and nurse the baby, which Marie-Anne and Clayton found both beautiful and shocking—the sight of their mother's hand on her swollen, blue-white breast, holding her flesh away from her baby's nose so that she could breathe. Then, they would hear the coffee grinder buzz in the kitchen and they would go up to get a coffee for their mother (they took turns) and help their father with the breakfast.

Sometimes, looking back on all that now, Marie-Anne felt as if someone had been telling her a continuous fairy story—or a long and beautiful lie. Or had she told it to herself? She couldn't remember any fights or arguments or accusations—those didn't start until *after*. She simply remembered a lot of happy times, important times—waking up from having her tonsils out and feeling awfully sick, but seeing her mother and father there, smiling at her, and the big cardboard box with the promised rollerskates on her bedside table. She remembered winter picnics at the beach, and family birthday parties where everybody got a present and the birthday person got to choose the menu and the kind of cake. She remembered a lot of laughing, always, and her father lying on the sofa, holding Patty up in the air, saying, "Oh God, I love this kid!" She did not remember her parents hugging or

12

kissing each other, but it did not seem strange at the time. She felt, she *knew* that there was a greal deal of love in the house; she always assumed that her parents loved one another. But that must have been different from "being in love." They had not "been in love" — or at least her father had not "been in love" with her mother. *Ever.* That meant that he was not attracted to her, that he did not want to hug and kiss her, that he did not want to make love to her. He was "in love" with Ardelle and he had never been "in love" before.

She remembered all the nice students who came once a week to her father's graduate seminar, who were always so good about cleaning up afterwards, so that there wouldn't be any extra work for her mother. Ardelle had been one of those students, last year. She was one of the most helpful; one of the last to leave.

So, when their mother announced one suppertime that her "mourning period" was over and she was damn well going to do something with her life, join Weight Watchers for starters, they all encouraged her and said that they'd help her stick to it and that they really didn't care if there were no more brownies or cheesecakes or apple fritters for a while. "Just until I get used to it," she said, "until I'm sure of my self-control." They were all built like their father, long and lean, and seemed to be able to eat anything, except that Clayton had to stay away from greasy foods or he got zits.

The next morning, Clayton taped up a sign to the refrigerator door:

*WEIGHT?*
*WAIT.*

And a little note from the *Guinness Book of Records* saying that the fattest man in the world had been buried in a piano case. Marie-Anne and Patty contracted to keep lots of raw vegetables in the fridge that had been prepared for snacks.

Their mother went every Thursday to the basement of the Scottish Auditorium on Fir Street and came back smiling each week. They got sick of roast turkey and tuna fish by the end of it, but she was so good and so determined that they never let on.

When she got home Thursday nights, she would sip herb tea and tell them funny stories about the other dieters. She told them how, if you weren't on Weight Watchers, you were called a "citizen" and how people stood up and told on themselves, when they'd been especially bad or good. "It was a bit like being in church," she said, and as with religion, the faithful were mostly women. She weighed everything on the little Weight Watchers scale which was kept on the counter by the stove. When she came home one Thursday night with her twenty-pound pin, they pooled their money and sent her a dozen red roses from "The Citizens." Clayton even offered to start jogging with her and they got up early so, they said, neither of them would feel embarrassed. Marie-Anne and Patty had breakfast ready when they returned.

In May, their mother learned that she had been accepted in the Education Department, so except for two weeks at the end of August — their father was teaching summer school that year — when they left her to go with him and Ardelle to Lac Le Jeune (for a camping holiday, a holiday which nobody enjoyed very much, although everybody tried, especially Ardelle), they spent the summer in the city, mostly at the beach, so that their mother could swot up a bit before term began. When they were delivered back after the camping trip, their father came in with them, while Ardelle waited in the car. "You look wonderful," he said to their mother. "I know," she said and they all laughed. She did not, however, invite him to sit down or to bring Ardelle in for a cup of coffee and, in spite of herself, Marie-Anne wondered how Ardelle felt, sitting out there in the car, waiting. She was wearing a sundress that made her look about Clayton's age and Marie-Anne realized, with a shock, that Ardelle was much closer in age to her brother than to her father. She wondered if Clayton had ever been "in love." He never brought girls to the house, and although he went to parties, she didn't think that he had ever taken a girl out alone. She couldn't imagine her brother fucking anybody; for that matter, she couldn't imagine her father fucking (in her mind, she quickly changed it to "making love to") her mother. But, she could imagine her father fucking Ardelle. Or rather, she could imagine him wanting to, if not actually "doing it." She wondered what it felt like and who would be the first man to fuck her. When they went to get school clothes, her mother said, "You're getting a nice figure, Marie-Anne," and she was pleased that her mother noticed. But often, her breasts hurt and she didn't like having her period because she was sure that the boys could tell.

After the first week of classes, her mother said, "Oh my God, I think I'm too old for all this!" So, they decided to take over a lot of the cooking and meal-planning and voted that they would go to Chinatown for dim-sum brunch on Sundays and just have sandwiches in the evenings.

Their father took Patty every other weekend and Marie-Anne was invited too, but she rarely went. Clayton went to visit on his own, and sometimes, he and his father went to a soccer game together or away fishing, without Ardelle.

Ardelle cut Patty's hair short and their mother was furious. She said that she had no right. But Clayton said, "Be reasonable, it looks great" — and it did. Sometimes when Clayton was off with his friends and Patty was away, Marie-Anne and her mother would make a huge pot of coffee and sit in bed on Saturday mornings, just chatting and relaxing. Marie-Anne was quick at school, so she never had much trouble with homework, but she was shy and found it difficult to make friends. If it hadn't been for her mother, she would have been very lonely on the weekends. "It will all come," her mother said. "I hated walking into class the first day and knowing that I was almost twenty years older than everybody else. And if you've been married a long time, well, you've been *protected*—from men, I mean. You could talk to them freely, because you weren't *free*. Now, there I am, single, or the next thing to it, and everytime I talk to a man, I think that *he* thinks I'm looking him over. It makes me very shy with men and a little defensive with the women, who are so much younger than I am, and some of them so obviously on the look-out for a man. I just tell myself to be patient, to stop measuring myself against other people — and maybe you have to do the same."

Sometimes, if everybody was home on Saturday night, they played Monopoly or Yahtzee or Hearts and sent out for pizza.

Now that their mother was past the thirty-pound mark, she could afford to cheat a little. Marie-Anne, who realized she had felt cold for over a year, began to feel warm again. She even thought about having a pajama party on her birthday, now that there was no more middle-of-the-night weeping. Birthday parties had always been strictly family, but she didn't think that they'd mind. Once in a while, she agreed to go out to a movie with her father, but only if he didn't bring Ardelle along. Once, he said, "I don't think you're being very fair, Marie-Anne," and she replied, "Oh, *fair*, what's that?" and burst into tears. He held her while she cried and murmured, "I love you, you know that I love you," over and over into her hair, but she would not be comforted and refused to "discuss" it with him.

Then, her mother met Lionel and the world came to an end. She announced one evening that she planned to have "a friend" over for dinner on Friday. They all had been very pleased, and, Marie-Anne realized later, they automatically assumed it was a woman. Marie-Anne answered the doorbell and when a tall red-haired man with a beard said, "You must be Marie-Anne," she stared at him blankly.

He had on an old brown suede jacket and blue jeans and yellow runners. "Didn't Helen tell you I was coming for dinner?"

She continued to stare at him, the door half-open, half-shut. Then, her mother ("*Helen*?" she thought. "Didn't *Helen* tell you?") came into the hall, saw the man and said, in a funny, phoney voice, "Oh, Lionel! I thought that maybe it was the paper boy! For God's sake, Marie-Anne, don't keep him standing on the porch!"

Within the month, he had moved in, not just into the house, but into their mother's bedroom. Marie-Anne thought that he was a creep—there was no other word for it—always creeping around in his runners and coming up behind you when you didn't expect it. He smoked a lot of dope, morning, noon and night, and he had a silly laugh, like a whinny, when he was stoned. Their mother began to smoke up with him, and often, Clayton as well; the whole house stank of marijuana. Sometimes, she would get home from school and find Patty already there, alone in the kitchen, drawing.

"Where's Mom? Not home yet?"

"She's upstairs. She and Lionel. They're tired. They're lying down."

It made Marie-Anne furious to think that her mother couldn't even bother to come downstairs and be there when Patty got home from school. Her mother and Lionel painted the bedroom a horrible Easter bunny purple and they locked the door when they were in there together. If Patty had a bad dream, she wasn't to go upstairs and disturb them; she was a big girl now. One night after supper, Patty announced that she wanted to come and spend the night with them.

"Not tonight," their mother said, smiling.

"When?"

"Oh, some time. It's not really healthy, you know, a big girl like you sleeping with her parents."

"*He's* not my parent!"

Mother was no longer smiling. "You know perfectly well what I mean."

Lionel was sitting at the end of the table with his usual stupid smile on his stupid face.

"Why don't you tell her the truth?" he said.

Mother looked at him nervously.

"What?"

"Why don't you tell her the TRUTH, for God's sake. Don't be so uptight about it."

"What truth?" Patty said. "What truth?"

Clayton was out to dinner at a friend's. Marie-Anne got up and began to clear the table. It was not her night, but she knew what was coming. The sobs in the middle of the night had been replaced by her mother's voice, low at first, a kind of moaning, then, louder and louder, until she was screaming. And then, a kind of choked laughter. And then, silence. She could not understand how Patty slept through it all.

"See," Lionel said, looking at Marie-Anne. "See how uptight your oldest daughter is. *You've* done that to her."

"Lionel!" Marie-Anne knew that her mother couldn't stop him, that he was enjoying the whole thing.

"Come on, Patty," she said. "Help me clear the table and I'll french-braid your hair."

"*What* truth?" Patty said.

"Your mother and I," Lionel said, "like to fuck at night — you know, *fuck!*" Here, he made a circle of his thumb and index finger and ran his other index finger through it, in and out. "Make love, do dirty things. We want to be alone when we do that. We don't want anybody else in our bed."

"Lionel!" Mother said again. Patty stood with the milk pitcher in her hand, not really understanding, her eyes full of tears.

"Come on," Marie-Anne said, "he's just being stupid."

She left the dishes for her mother to deal with and took her sister downstairs.

"Daddy and Mommy used to let me sleep in their bed," Patty said.

"I know. He's just being horrible."

"I wish that he'd go away. I hate him."

Marie-Anne got Patty into her nightgown and slippers and braided her hair, while they watched television. They could hear Lionel and their mother having a terrific row in the kitchen.

"Maybe she'll kick him out," Patty said. "Maybe she'll get so mad at him that she'll tell him to get lost."

But she didn't; Marie-Anne knew that she wouldn't. Instead, she had a long talk with the two girls the next afternoon, told them how important her relationship with Lionel was, how happy he made her feel, how he had given her a new life, really, and how it was awfully difficult for him to walk into a ready-made family. She explained how her own relationship with them had become rather unhealthy, "almost incestuous," she said and laughed — and Patty looked puzzled. "It was too easy," she explained, "none of us had to go outside the home for our emotional fulfillment. I was sad and lonely, and so, I *used* you all, *leant* on you too much. Now, we have to be a little more separate." At the end of it all, she asked them to call her Helen.

"She's not a *real* mother anymore," Patty said one day. "She doesn't love anybody but that jerk Lionel."

"That's not true," Marie-Anne said. Their mother had forgotten

18

to give Patty money for her field trip three days in a row. "She's very busy. She goes to school, too, you know, as well as being our mother."

"Daddy and Ardelle let me sleep in their bed," Patty said. Marie-Anne just smiled and changed the subject, but she thought to herself, "They have all week alone." She wasn't really on her mother's side; she detested Lionel and his superior manner and she thought that he wasn't worthy of her mother. He reminded her more of some creepy high school boy than a twenty-eight year old man. And she hated the way that he talked to Patty, calling her a "fucking little bitch" if she dared to stand up to him at all, or interrupted him to ask her mother something. Sometimes, he would ask the meaning of some word that he'd heard Patty use, when he could tell perfectly well that she'd only just heard it and wanted to try it out. "Yes, dear," he would say, "but what does it *mean*?" If you asked him what time it was, he went into a long discussion of relative time versus absolute time (things like that), while you stood there, wanting to scream. He wouldn't allow any sugar in the house, or cookies or cake, and he said that he really wasn't sure, but what he thought they should do is give up meat. Meat only made you aggressive. Marie-Anne and Patty kept a supply of goodies hidden in their room. She was sure that their mother knew about them, but she didn't want to cause any more trouble. Their mother didn't come down to their room very often any more, and when she did, she didn't stay. Instead of tucking Patty in and kissing her, she would run down the stairs, see them side by side watching television, and say, "Oh well, since you're so comfy, I won't disturb you. I'll say goodnight now." Once, she came down, just as Marie-Anne was tucking Patty in and she said, "Sometimes, I think that you're the mother and I'm the teenager, Marie-Anne!" She waited until Marie-Anne got into her own bed, then she reached up to turn off the light. Marie-Anne could see all the silvery stretch marks on her mother's belly. It made her feel sick.

Patty spent nearly every weekend with their father now, and sometimes, Marie-Anne would go with them to a movie or to Stanley Park, but she always refused to spend the night. Ardelle

19

was pregnant; she wondered if her mother knew. Clayton liked Lionel because he let him come up to his room and listen to his stereo on the headset and he gave him free joints and talked to him about being a star runner in high school. On the weekends, Marie-Anne really missed Patty and she often said that she wasn't hungry, or that she was going to make herself a sandwich later, rather than eat with the other three. Once, Lionel came up behind her in the kitchen and put his arms around her waist.

"Get your filthy hands off me!" she said.

"Oh, excuse *me*," he said. "Next time, I'll wash my hands."

"There won't be a next time," she said, keeping her back to him.

"What do you mean by *that*, Marie-Anne?"

She didn't know what she meant. She was so miserable that she wanted to die.

One weekend, Lionel and her mother gave a "Come As You Were" party for all their friends. Her mother had to let it out a bit, but she wore her wedding dress, and so she wouldn't be taken too seriously, some sweet-pea netting for a veil. Lionel was going as a track star and he said that he was going to run around the block ten times just before the party, so that he'd smell just right. Clayton was going to help with the drinks and get paid for it, but when they asked Marie-Anne if she'd like to earn some money as a waitress, she said, "No thanks," so her mother suggested that she spend the weekend at her father's with Patty, but she hadn't wanted to do that either. She didn't know what she wanted to do. She went upstairs to get a bowl of chili, just before the party began. Lionel was sitting in his shorts at the table, rolling joints. His chest was covered with curly rust-coloured hair. She had to reach across him in order to get a bowl from the cupboard.

"Not going to join us, Princess?"

She didn't bother to reply and that made him mad. He grabbed the bowl from her hand.

"Since you aren't willing to help or be civil, I don't see why you should have any of our chili. The chili's for the party, not for spoiled brats." He tipped her dinner back into the pot.

Trembling, she reached up for another bowl.

"I *mean* it, Marie-Anne." He grabbed her wrist.

"Let me alone, please." Her voice was trembling so hard that she could hardly recognize it as her own.

"You're *chilly* enough, Marie-Anne. You don't need it." He laughed hard at his own stupid joke. "You know what the trouble with you is, you're jealous. You're jealous of your mother's happiness and it's twisting you all up inside. It's making you sick."

She was so angry that his face wavered and danced in front of her. If she could have reached the knives, she would gladly have killed him. But the doorbell rang and he let her go. She fled downstairs.

That night, supperless, miserable, she lay on her bed in a kind of fever. The music thudded over her head and there was a lot of laughter and noise. It seemed to her that she could no longer stay here. But she didn't want to go without Patty—and go where? She had no money. Her grandparents were thousands of miles away.

Just before dawn, she fell asleep and had a strange dream that all the people upstairs were dancing on enormous black and white squares of polished marble, and that, suddenly, they began to slip and slide, and all their legs broke off at the ankles. She could hear the screams, the screams, the screams.

The next day, before anyone surfaced, she got up and got dressed and took the bus to her father's apartment. He and Ardelle and Patty were eating breakfast and were quite surprised to see her.

"Marie-Anne!" her father said. "Come in and have some pancakes." Ardelle got up from the table and smiled at her.

"I have to talk to you," Marie-Anne said. "I have to talk to you alone." Then, she burst into tears.

Her father drew her inside and shut the door. "It's all right," he said. "It's going to be all right."

She did not tell her mother where she had been or what she had done, but a week later, her father phoned and he and her mother arranged to meet. Marie-Anne watched her mother, very jaunty, very pretty, in a new pantsuit and high-heeled boots, set off for the appointment. Marie-Anne went and threw up in the downstairs toilet.

It snowed early that year and on the morning when her father came to get them, there was quite a lot of snow on the ground. Her mother was still in her dressing gown and she had been crying. Marie-Anne told Patty to get in the front seat, in the middle, and that she'd sit by the door. She could see her mother's face in the sitting-room window. Then, suddenly, just as the car began to pull away from the curb, her mother dashed down the front steps, barefoot in the snow, her dressing gown open, screaming at them, pounding on the car window, running after the car and shouting, "Don't take my baby from me, don't take my baby from me, don't take...."

# NATURAL HISTORY

Something had run over her hand. Now she was wide awake and sitting up, the sleeping bag flung off, her heart pounding. What? The rat? No, don't be foolish — a mouse maybe, a vole, perhaps just the cat's tail swishing, as she came back to see if they were still persisting in this out-of-doors foolishness when there were all those comfortable beds and cushions inside. Clytie tried to get the cat to lie down at their feet, but it walked away.

"She probably thinks we're nuts," the mother said.

"Maybe she'll jump in the bathroom window and wait for us to come whining and begging to be let in."

"And she'll say, 'Well, my dears, now you know what it feels like when *I* want in'."

The cat was old, but very independent, except for wanting to sleep inside at night. They often spoke for her, having endowed her with the personality of a querulous, but rather imperious, old woman.

"Maybe she'll do us the favour of catching that rat," she added.

"You *know* that she won't," the child said. "She's afraid."

"She's not afraid; she's lazy."

But something would have to be done. No mouse could have gnawed a hole like that, right through the outside of the cottage and into the cupboard, under the sink, where the compost bucket was kept. A hole the size of a man's fist. They never saw the rat, but they heard it when they were lying in bed in the other room; and last night, it was on the roof, or rather, *in* the roof, directly over their heads. A determined *chewing* sound. They both woke up.

"I hope that it electrocutes itself on a wire."

"Do they really eat people?"

"No. Some of those old tales from Europe were probably based on fact. Maybe in times of famine—or when it was very cold. Maybe then. But these rats come off the fishboats; they're not starving. Rats are just big mice; there's no real biological difference." So she spoke to reassure her daughter, but nevertheless, they lay awake in the big double bed, holding hands, not liking the idea of a long, narrow, whiskered face suddenly appearing through the ceiling. Something would have to be done. She thought of rabies; she even thought of the plague. This morning, she had gone down to the store to see if they carried rat poison.

"Not any more," the storekeeper said. "We used to, but they won't let us any more.... Because we sell food," he added. "In case something spilled, I guess."

So, they'd have to take a trip to town and find a drugstore. Would they look at her strangely? She thought of Emma Bovary asking for arsenic. She said that she wanted to kill some rats that were keeping her awake. Cramming it into her mouth. Ugh. She would see if it were possible to get enough for only one rat. She came back up the path discouraged. She didn't want to go anywhere. She just wanted to stay here with her child and complete her recovery. Nice word that, re-cover. To cover yourself over again, something essential having been ripped away, like a deep rip in the upholstery. Then there had been the visitors to think about.

They were not sleeping outside because of the rat, but in spite of it. They were sleeping outside because of the full moon. They had talked about the moon for days. If it were fine ("And when wasn't it fine, over here, in July?" they asked each other), they would sleep out and watch the moon rise. And so, after supper, they carried out pillows and sleeping bags, a thermos of coffee and some cookies, in case they woke up early in the morning; and they made themselves a nest under the apple trees. The apples were still small and green, hardly distinguishable from the leaves. They were winter apples. There was a woven hammock that had been slung between two of the trees. She had rigged up a rope, thrown it over a stout branch and tied it, at the other end of the hammock, to a discarded wooden toy, so that one could lie in the hammock and reach up and gently rock oneself.

"The ultimate in laziness," she said. They took turns lying in the hammock, reading, the other one stretched out on an old blanket nearby.

But the moon had taken so long, so long that, first, the little girl had given a great sigh and turned over, backed up into the warmth of her mother, with her face away from the moon's rising, and slept; and then, the mother, too, slept.

But the mother was now wide awake, with the moon, high and white; and the moonlight falling over on the far side, hitting a white shed that lay beyond the house. Was it moving away from them or towards them? she wondered. Old wives' tales came back to her, about not letting the moonlight strike your face—and the memory of the blind girl that they had met that day, with her round, vacant, staring eyes. Ugh. Too many morbid thoughts.

She got up quietly and walked away a little bit to pee, squatting in the long grass. She had borrowed a scythe from a neighbour up the road, a real old-fashioned scythe, with a long wooden handle and a curved, vicious blade, and had found that, once she got the hang of it, she liked the rhythm of the thing, walking forward, moving her hips just so or the blade wouldn't cut clean, it simply hacked or flattened out the grass; but when they went to pick up the grass, they found that it was still fastened to the earth. She hadn't come around to this side yet with the scythe—perhaps tomorrow. The night was utterly still; even the owl, which they heard so often, but had never seen, was silent. And there was no breeze, except that, every so often, a ripple would pass through the firs, the alders, the pear tree and the apple trees which almost surrounded the house. It was as

25

though the night itself were an animal, a huge dark cat which twitched and quivered from time to time in its sleep.

"I should sell this place by moonlight," she thought. "Then no one would notice the peeling paint or the cracked windowpanes or the impossible angle of the chimney."

"Describe this house," the blind girl had said, eagerly. "What does it look like?"

"It looks like a witch's house," Clytie said, without hesitation, "like something that a witch might live in." She was showing off—they had been reading Grimm's fairytales—but still, her mother was hurt.

"It's very beautiful," the blind girl's companion said. "The wall that you are leaning against is a lovely mustard-yellow and the couch that we are sitting on is purple."

"What sort of purple?"

"Very nearly the purple of that shawl you bought in Guadalajara."

So, she hadn't been blind long. Not long ago, she had seen and bought a purple shawl in a Mexican market. The girl—a young woman really—was terribly overweight and that, too, seemed recent. There was something about the way that she moved her body, or moved *in* her body, like a child all bundled up. Diabetes. Lifting the teapot, the mother's hand turned cold. The blindness, as well as the fatness, were merely signs that things inside had got out of control. What was the word? She had heard it often enough. "Stabilize." They hadn't, yet, been able to "stabilize" the disease. A seeing-eye dog, a magnificent golden Labrador, lay at the blind girl's feet. A plate of cookies was offered. They had been mixed and baked deliberately for their variety of texture: oatmeal cookies, chocolate chip, hermits. "If I'd only known," she thought. But it was interesting. Once again, the blind girl asked for visual description before she made her choice; indeed, she hardly touched the cookies at all.

Clytie watched every move, fascinated. The girl told them that she was writing poems. "Trying to get some of my anger out," she said with a little laugh. Perhaps she wanted to be asked to recite.

"We're sleeping outside tonight," Clytie said, "under the

moon." The girl laughed again, the laugh too small for her large, awkward body. "Be careful not to look at a reflection of the moon in water," she said. "It's very dangerous to do that."

"Why?"

"I think that you're supposed to go mad."

Another old wives' tale.

And there was the moon now—silent, indifferent, unaware of all the myths and tales and proverbs which she had inspired! Words too, like lunatic, moony. The other day, she said to her daughter, "Stop mooning around and *do* something." As though the moon were aimless or haphazard when, in reality, she was so predictable, so orderly, that her passages could be predicted with extreme accuracy. "July 19th: Perigee moon occurs only six hours before full moon." Growing, brightening, reaching fullness; waning, dimming, beginning the whole thing over again. The old triple moon goddess, corresponding to the three phases of woman. Her little girl, Clytie, named not for the moon, but after the sunflower, was very orderly. She had drawn up a schedule at the beginning of the summer and taped it to the refrigerator door. They were going to have to work hard in the garden, yes. They were also going to have periods when each would wish to be alone, agreed; when one or the other would go out to the old shed and work on some private thing. They were going to start a study of intertidal creatures; they were going to paint the kitchen; they were going to learn the names of the con-stellations. There it all was, on the refrigerator door, all worked out—a calendar of orderly and edifying progression through the long summer, decorated in the corners with orange suns and pur-ple starfish.

And there it remained, because things hadn't quite worked out like that. For one thing, it had been very hot; for another, they both seemed to have been overtaken with a kind of lethargy: the child, probably because she was growing so fast; the mother, perhaps because she was unwilling to really "come to" and think about the future.

They had worked hard during the winter, getting up at 6 a.m. and lighting fires, leaving time for a good breakfast before the yellow school bus came. And they went to bed early as well. If

27

someone rang after 9 p.m., one or the other had to crawl out of bed in the dark to answer the phone.

She was writing a book and she worked all day while her daughter was away at school. She sat next to the wood stove, the cat asleep on a chair beside her. The simple life: it was what she craved and what she needed. On weekends, they did the wash in the old wringer-washer, shoving the clothes through the wringer with a wooden spoon; they baked bread and cookies, stacked wood, read books and listened to the radio.

"It seems so peaceful here!" the blind girl cried, as they sat in the front room, sipping tea and nibbling cookies. "It must be paradise to be here all year round."

Paradise: "a walled garden, an enclosure." Disaster: "a turning away from the stars."

The blind girl was from Los Angeles. Her companion, older, rather stern-faced until she smiled, was the niece of one of the earliest families on the island. "She wants so much to meet you," the woman said on the phone. "I have been reading your poems to her. It would mean a great deal to her."

She did not want to meet anyone, especially anyone who had suffered, who was perhaps suffering still, but she could think of no graceful way to get out of it. It hadn't been too bad, really. She wondered and worried about her daughter's reaction, but the child seemed more interested than alarmed.

"9 a.m.: exercises, bike-riding," the schedule announced, as they sat at the kitchen table in their nightgowns, eating scones and strawberry jam. "Two hours a day, intertidal life," it called down to them from where they dozed on the rocks, the green notebook — they were still on seaweed — neglected at the bottom of the towel. They painted each other's toes and fingernails impossible colours, and waved their hands and feet in the air to dry. They timed each other to see who could stay the longest in the icy water. The yellow paint for the kitchen remained in the shed while they lay on the hammock and the blanket and read *The Wind in the Willows* out loud.

"You can't help liking Toad," Clytie said. "I know that I shouldn't like him, but I do."

Strange little creatures done up in leggings and waistcoats, thinking our kinds of thoughts and feeling our emotions. "The English were particularly good at that," she thought. "And look at me, pretending the cat will pass moral judgment on our sleeping arrangements, and feeling that, any second now, I'll see her up in a tree, grinning."

But the rat was real. The rat would have to be dealt with. "The cat takes the rat," she thought, "but maybe only in the rhyme."

Sometimes, they drove down to the other end of the island to a sandy beach where the water was warmer, and they spent the afternoon and early evening there. Last week, there had been several young women sitting on the beach with their babies and watching their older children swim. She got into a discussion with a woman that she knew slightly, whom she hadn't seen in months. The woman was very beautiful, with curly dark hair and long dancer's legs. It turned out that her husband had left her and the children to go and live with a younger woman. "I'm better now," she said, "but I spent a month thinking up ways to kill him — to kill them both. Really."

"I believe you," she said. "Last winter, I chopped kindling every day. It wasn't kindling, of course, it was hands and fingers and lips; ears, eyes, private parts. Everything chopped up small and thrown into the stove. We were as warm as toast."

"I'm glad to hear somebody else admit to such feelings," the other woman said, laughing.

"What are all those operas about, those myths, those 'crimes of passion'? We just aren't open about it in these northern climates."

"He says that he can do so much for her," the other woman said.

(And the moon up there, female, shining always by reflected light, dependent on the sun, yet so much brighter, seemingly, against the darkness of the sky; so much more mysterious, changing her shape, controlling the waters, gathering it all in her net.)

It was dark when they drove back up the island and the eyes of the deer glowed yellow-gold in the headlights. Once or twice, they saw a raccoon with eyes like emeralds.

29

"Why don't our eyes do that at night?"

"I don't understand it completely," she said. "It's because those animals go out at night. They have something like a mirror, maybe like your bike reflector, at the back of the eye. This gives them a second chance to use whatever light there is. It hits the mirror and bounces back again. Then, what's left over shines out. 'Wasted light,' I think it's called. Your grandfather taught me all that stuff. He knew all about it, but he wasn't very good at explaining it, or at least not to me. Maybe he was just tired or maybe I wasn't very good at listening. I can still remember him trying to explain about the sun and moon, one Saturday morning, when I was about your age. I don't think that I *asked* him; I think that he just wanted to explain it! He had an orange, a grapefruit, a flashlight and a pencil. He stuck a pencil through the grapefruit for the earth on its axis, but I got terribly lost. I stood on one foot and then the other, and finally, I asked if I could go out and play. I think that he was terribly hurt."

The blind girl told stories about her dog. She made everything gay and light and witty. Once, she and another blind friend had taken their dogs into a posh Los Angeles restaurant. "It's against the law to keep us out," she explained. It was the friend's birthday, so they saved up their money to go out together and celebrate. The waiter was very helpful and they ordered a fancy meal. Their dogs lay quiet and well-behaved beneath the table. Everybody felt good.

"Then, Samson sort of sat up—I could feel him. He gave a sigh and did a huge shit, right by my chair. It was *so* awful. We could hear the people who were nearest to us, saying, 'Well, *really,*' and similar things. The smell was very powerful and we got hysterical. We were laughing our heads off at the whole idea. We could sort of 'feel' the maître d' hovering nearby, uncertain whether or not to kick these gross blind people out and maybe face some sort of lawsuit, or lose all his patrons; or just try to ignore the whole thing, pick up the poop and carry on."

"What happened?" At the mention of his name, the dog sat up, wagging his tail, as though he, too, were enjoying the story.

"Well, I carefully lowered my big, beautiful, starched dinner napkin, over where I thought the pile was—I didn't actually want to get my fingers in it—and then I called out: 'Waiter, waiter. I'm afraid my dog has had a little accident'."

"But we never went back there," she added when they stopped laughing. "Never."

"I would not have offered cookies," she thought, "if I had known. I would not have *tempted* her, especially with homemade cookies, offered by the young girl who had home-made them." The man who tried to teach her about the motions of the sun and moon and earth on its axis had been a diabetic too, or had become one, only much later in life than their visitor. He could not give up all the sweet rich foods that he loved. He was dead now; he did not even know that she had a child. "Just this once," he used to say, as he put sugar on his grapefruit, or ordered a dish of chocolate ice-cream. And her mother, joining in, would say, "Oh, it won't hurt him, just this once." He had been quite short-sighted and the thing that made her realize how dead he was, was, after the funeral, finding his bifocals in a drawer. How many cookies had the blind girl eaten? She couldn't remember.

"I don't really feel lonely any more," she said to her friend on the beach. "I used to. I used to think that I'd die from loneliness, as if it were a disease. I suppose that I'll want to be with someone again, but right now, I'm content. Only, some days—when the fucking clothesline breaks or I'm down to the wet wood, things like that—I wish that there were someone around. But then, I ask myself, 'Is it a husband that I want or a hired hand'?"

"A hired hand might be useful for other things as well."

"Or a hired finger." They giggled.

(He would have dealt with this rat, for instance. He would have got rid of it quick.)

One night, the cat caught a mouse and started munching it in the darkness of the room where she and Clytie were sleeping.

"*Really*," she said, waking up and recognizing what was going on.

And Clytie, laughing, got up in her long white nightdress and threw the cat outside.

She wasn't the least afraid of that. But she was terrified to be alone in the dark, as her mother had been terrified when she was

31

a child, as perhaps all children were terrified of the dark. Which is why she sat here, now, wide awake and thoughtful, her half of the sleeping bag over her knees, rather than inside the house, sipping a cup of tea and reading until she became sleepy again.

They had done away with mousetraps because they couldn't stand that awful, final "click."

"Ugh," the child said, crawling back in bed, "that crunching sound was really *disgusting*." And they both began to laugh.

"Shall we make her a mouse pie the next time she does that?"

"Would you? Would you really?"

"Why not?"

"It might smell terrible."

"Would you really make a mouse pie with a crust, like in *The Pie and the Pattypan*?"

"Oh God, I don't know.... Probably not."

They caught a rock cod near the government wharf and when they cleaned it and removed the stomach, there were three small crabs inside.

"I suppose that they have some sort of acid in their stomachs which dissolves the shell," she said.

"I guess everything just goes around eating everything else," her child said.

"Sometimes it seems that way."

The blind girl turned her head towards whomever was speaking; she turned towards the sound. The sunflower, Clytie, following her beloved Apollo as he crossed the sky. The moon, shining always with reflected light.

"Where are all the strong men," the woman on the beach said, "now that there are all these strong women?"

("I'm getting awfully symbolic out here, wide awake beneath the moon." The absolute trust of her sleeping child moved her almost to tears. She would sit here all night, if necessary; it didn't matter.)

"I can't stay on this island forever," she thought. "I will end up like an old witch in a witch's cottage. I've got to give my life some serious attention. It's all very well to sit around reading fairytales and making a game of everything." She glanced at her daughter's long hair which was spread out on the pillow beside her. "*She'll* change; maybe she'll change first. She'll want more than this." Her namesake, turned into a sunflower, gazing blindly towards the sun. The moon (female), shining always by his light.

("Let her be strong," she thought. "Let her be strong and yet still loving." A few years ago, in the city, she had come home from school and announced, at dinner, that a policeman had come to the school and given a talk about "strangers." Her mother and father glanced quickly at one another. A little girl, her lunchbox beside her, had been found dead in a ditch.

"And what are strangers?" asked her father gently, curious as to what she had been told, yet wanting to keep the story light.

The child's reply was very serious.

"Strangers are usually men.")


"Dis-aster," they read in the dictionary: "a falling away from the stars." "Paradise," from the Persian: "a walled garden." "*Lunaticus*" f. L., "affected by the moon." And who had first made *that* connection? Galileo. He built his "optik glasse" and discovered that the moon (female, shining always with reflected light) was not the "luminous orb" of the poets, but rather, full of "vast protuberances, deep chasms and sinuosities."

Later, in England, men looked at a flea through a microscope and saw "the devil shut up in a glasse." Mankind was always wanting more, wanting to make far things nearer, small things larger; to know and understand it all. When the Americans stepped on the moon, one of her friends had written a long mock-heroic poem called "The Rape of Cynthia."

The trick was, of course, to try and get the right distance on everything; to stand in just the right relationship to it all. But how? Would her daughter be any better at it than she was? Another image came to mind, out of her childhood, a stereopticon belonging to her grandfather. She would sit with it, on a Sunday afternoon, sliding the crossbar up and down, until suddenly, "click," the two photographs taken at slightly different angles (St. Mark's, the Tower of London, Notre Dame) would become one picture, which would take on depth and a wonderful illusion of solidity. *That* was the trick. To slide it all—moon, blind girl, rat, the apple tree, her father's fingers tilting the pencil, her own solitude, the cat, the eyes of the deer, her daughter, this still moment, back/forth, back/forth, back/forth, until "click,"

until "click,"

until "click"—

there it was: wholeness, harmony, radiance; all of it making a wonderful kind of sense, as she sat there under the apple tree, beneath the moon.

And then, suddenly, because she *did* see, if only for an instant, she bent down and she shielded the child's body as the moonlight, finally, reached them.


"What amazes me," Clytie said, just before she turned over and went to sleep, "is that we're just part of a system. We're all just floating around."

# GALATEA

*A picture must be built up by means of rhythm, calculation and selection.*

Sentence found in a guidebook
in the Jeu de Paume

Two swans went down the river, but only one came back. The phrase kept repeating itself, over and over, the opening sentence of a fairytale or the beginning of some problem in algebra: Swan A and Swan B, moving at different speeds.

But they weren't. She had been lying on the bed, with her eyes shut, listening to the sound of the river coming in through the open windows, almost a rustling sound today, almost a dry sound, rather than wet. She had been asking herself whether or not she would have recognized that sound, if she had not known it was a river. Would she not have thought that it was the sound of dry leaves in a forest?

That was last Friday. As she lay there, with her eyes closed, Peter called to her from the other room: "Look out your window at the swans." And there they were, gliding past the vegetable garden at the back of the hotel, with their long snaky necks held high, their bills turned slightly towards one another, as though they were two travellers on one of those moving sidewalks that you find in big airport terminals, having a chat, wondering if they had remembered to bring the address book. "Perhaps they're off for an illicit weekend in Bergerac," she called to him, and he laughed. The river was running fast, and soon the swans were no more than two slightly soiled-looking white specks.

But, just now, kneeling on the windowseat and staring down at the river, trying to memorize the particular shade of milky green that it was at this moment (it was always some shade of green, although, in the postcards that she bought at the *tabac,* it was invariably blue), she saw a solitary swan coming up the river, heading towards the bridge. It need not be one of the swans that they saw on Friday, of course—there was a single swan who lived in the pond at the centre of town, and there might have been some way that he could have got to the river via the canal—yet that phrase popped into her head, as soon as she saw him: "Two swans went down the river, but only one came back." She wanted to knock on the wall and ask Peter if swans mate for life; it was the sort of thing that he would know. He knew all kinds of things like that: the seven principal rivers of the world, the six tallest buildings, the year in which Darwin wrote *The Origin of Species.* He devoured dictionaries and encyclopedias; he said that it was simply a form of knowledge for its own sake, and besides, you never knew when something might come in handy.

She didn't knock, however; she didn't want to disturb him. For the past hour, she listened to him clear his throat at regular intervals, a curious habit that he had, which usually meant that his work was going well. The afternoon had been so relaxed, she was surprised that he could work at all. Afternoons were supposed to be uneventful: a stroll along the canal, lunch and a chat by the pond; a walk across the bridge and up to one of the marked footpaths, which took them through oak forests and fields that were pitted with animal hooves, past small villages with farmhouses that were made of stone. Seeing the poppies among the wheat and corn, they agreed that, for the first time, they really "saw" the poem that they had both been made to memorize as children. They would come back from these outings, relaxed and pleasantly fatigued, and they would go to their rooms—he, to work; she, to sketch or nap—until he would knock on her door and they would have a drink in her room, before going down to dinner—she, sipping on a pastis ("God," said Peter, "I don't know how you can drink that stuff!"); he, on a Scotch and water. Or maybe two. They did not take their drinks on the *terrasse,* ostensibly because the weather had been a bit chilly, but really because, considering the amount that they drank, it was much cheaper to buy by the bottle. Tonight, she felt like going down by herself, not waiting for him, but she knew that he would be hurt. It was really only to get rid of that sentence that was going around in her head, to replace it with other sentences (living with him all these years had taught her to be a good eavesdropper), to perhaps chat with little Pierre for a while. Pierre was out on the *terrasse* and his high thin voice drifted up, with the smells of dinner cooking—onions and other comfortable aromas. They always had the *menu fixe* (it was included in their weekly rent), but this being their last night there, they were going to choose the more expensive menu—and have pâté de fois grâs besides. "And champagne," Peter said. "If I'm finished or near the end, we'll have champagne."

"You'll finish," she said stoutly, not really believing it, but loving him so much and knowing that he needed her to say it. "Behind every successful artist," the wife of one of Peter's colleagues said once, "stands a surprised wife." She had been shocked, then, by the woman's cynicism. She was still shocked, but now she understood a little bit more about it. This same woman went around at cocktail parties explaining that her husband, somewhere along the line, had to make a choice between being a great poet and being a good father, and he had chosen the latter. "If he had had it in him to be a great poet," Peter said, "there wouldn't have been any choice."

"Do you mean to say that he couldn't have wanted children?"

"No," he said (this was several years ago). "I don't mean that. Or I don't think that I mean that. Greatness always seems, to me, to be like one of those magic pitchers in a fairytale—you pour it out and it is still full to the top. I'm interested in the distinction that she always makes between the great poet and the good father. If a man were genuinely great, he might not be a 'good' father, by conventional standards, but his greatness would be bound to influence his children. Just to be exposed to a mind like that!"

"There might not be the time," she said.

"?"

"He might not want to spare the time to 'expose' them."

"Nonsense," he said. "Just by being in the same house with him, sitting down to dinner with him, they would be 'exposed.' Just by breathing the same air!"

"And who would look after them when they were 'exposed' to other things that were less beneficial?" she said, half-teasing, half-serious. "Mumps, for instance. Or chicken pox."

"Why, the great man's wife, of course. Who did you think?" He nibbled her ear.

On the small, local train from Limoges to Perigueux, they sat next to a man and his wife who were very old. The old man had "death spots," as her mother used to call them, on the backs of his hands. The old woman sat next to her, a small Dachshund on her lap. She was most anxious to assure them that one lived well in France. She turned coy at one point and asked them to guess her age. The dog, who was old and very quiet, was passed gently from the wife to the husband. "Il est sage," the old man said, when they remarked on the dog's good behaviour. "He is wise." They had never had any children. "Hélas," said the old woman, smiling.

She could go for a walk, but no, she might not be back when he was ready for his aperitif. She might not be there when he needed her. The second morning, with the sound of the river and the birds enticing her outside, she walked along the canal by herself. Two old men sat on the bank, fishing with long bamboo poles. She passed a chicken farm, an old people's home and a water rat, coming quietly up onto the bank, his wet fur glistening in the sun. She walked a long way before she found a footbridge that she could cross to get to the other side. On the low cement wall of the footbridge, someone had written a message in chalk: "Je suis obligée d'aller à Bergerac. Sylvie." The message looked fresh. She was tempted to wait and see who would show

38

up. She had her sketchbook with her, always a legitimate excuse for loitering. (Peter sometimes used her that way, when he wanted to overhear conversations.) But, she crossed the footbridge and began to walk back into town, hurrying a little as she heard the cathedral clock strike one. Another clock, which they had not yet located, came in a few seconds later. She called them the "M'sieu-Dame" clocks, for everywhere that they strolled in this region, people greeted them with: "Bonjour, M'sieu-Dame," "Bonsoir, M'sieu-Dame," as though it were all one word—but always the man first and the woman slightly behind, as was only proper. The "M'sieu" clock even cleared his throat before striking. It reminded her of Peter and she told him so, not with any malice, for she had long ago accepted that she would always walk a little behind this brilliant, articulate man, who, through some miracle, happened to be her husband. When the more militant females in Peter's department came to dinner and admired her sketches (Peter always insisted that she bring them out), when they asked her why she didn't "do" something with her talent, she just laughed and said, "Oh, I'm just a dabbler!" When they insisted that she could be more than that, if she'd just *work* at it, she would surprise them by turning quite cold and changing the subject. She did not like these women, but she was neither afraid of them nor intimidated by them. Not any more. When they first decided to come to France, she looked up the word in her pocket Larousse, just in case anyone should ask. To dabble: "S'occuper un peu de _____." "Je m'occupe un peu de _____." A duck, not a swan.

She brought him back a nosegay from her walk: white daisies, yellow buttercup-like flowers, Queen Anne's lace, and blue flowers that she didn't recognize, rather like harebells. (She had picked one for herself and pressed it in her sketchbook.) He accepted the bouquet rather ungraciously, for he had knocked off early and had been waiting for her.

"You've got grass stains on your trousers," he said.

"They'll come out." And, by way of apology, she offered him the two old men fishing, with their long poles just inches above the water, the yellow irises, the old people, like ancient flowers, sitting out on benches, with their faces turned to the sun. For some reason, which she did not understand, she decided to keep the message from Sylvie to herself, and when next she walked along the canal, this time with her husband, she noticed that the message had been rubbed out.

The paintings that she had done during the one terrible year when he left her, had been praised by her teacher, large canvases full of brutal colours. But they frightened her; it was as though she had hung herself up there on the wall. After they were back together, they discussed it. "I don't see why I should hang these up," she said. "Why should I display myself like that?" He agreed. She knew that the paintings frightened him too. He never saw her as a violent person, as someone who just might possibly kill. It frightened him and it moved him. He put his arms around her. "Whatever you say. But could I have something of yours for my study?" They were moving to a new city, a new job. ("You can come back," she told him, "but I do not want to stay here. It's up to you.") So, he kept a less disturbing painting above his desk — she had gone back to watercolours and had abandoned oils and acrylics — a painting of some Chinese women that she had seen once in a large field outside Vancouver, bending over, picking something. They wore enormous straw hats to shield them from the sun. She was fascinated by the decorative aspect of their bent forms — under their hats, against the August sun. For the first time, she felt that she had been able to get outside of "content," to simply see the women as part of the landscape, not to be concerned that their backs hurt or how much they were getting an hour. It made her understand something about Peter, too, how he could use friends, or relatives even, as well as other "real" people, in his novels and stories. He told her that it was one of the best things that she had ever done.

At the Gare d'Austerlitz, he asked her to take a picture of him walking towards the train. She was to wait until he had gone about twenty-five yards, then click the shutter. As she watched him through the viewfinder, her hands began to shake. He was walking away from her. "Don't be silly," she said to herself, but she pressed the button quickly and she knew that the picture probably wouldn't turn out.

Two swans went down the river, but only one came back.

"I've fallen in love with the river," she said to Peter on the last night, as they leaned on the yellow stone bridge and looked back at their hotel. "Are there any myths about girls falling in love with rivers?"

"I don't think so," he said. "It's usually the River God who pursues the nymph."

They rented a car at Perigueux, hoping that if they drove for a few days, they would come to the perfect village in which Peter could work for their last two weeks, and where they could "stay put" and get a real sense of the countryside. They loved Paris, but it had worn them out. Their first night with the car, they found a beautiful inn, mentioned in their *Auberges et Relais,* high above the river, and aptly named, "Le Beau Regard." After supper, the patron told them that they should drive up to the *cinglé* and watch the sunset. While they were looking down over the fields below them, the broad silver river as smooth as a piece of sheet metal, no sound, but the sound of birds, the angelus began to ring. "Angelus Domini," Peter said. "Oh, my God, I didn't know people still lived like this." He had tears in his eyes.

"Shall we stay here forever?" she said.

He smiled down at her. "And live on what, Madame?"

"This is going to be 'the' book, remember?"

They wanted to climb the look-out tower, but it was locked.

"Incarnadine," he said that night, writing in his notebook.

"What does that mean?"

"Crimson. But it can mean flesh-coloured. I don't think, ever before, that I've seen such a flesh-coloured sky." He sighed. "I wish that I were a poet."

"Why? Or why, right now?"

"Oh. Well, something came back to me, although I haven't been inside a church in years—except to look at it, I mean. The angelus commemorates the Incarnation, the Word made flesh. And then, that sky, that wonderful rosy, flesh-coloured sky. A poet could make good use of all that."

"And you can't?"

"Oh, not really. You know that I'm not good at that sort of thing."

(Which was true. He was no good at settings. In fact, she

41

often "did" them for him. He would tell her what a character was like and she would create the setting. She enjoyed it. It was like being a set designer.

"She would have a cupboard full of high-heeled shoes. That would be her one real extravagance. Because of her ankles."

"How do you know that she has nice ankles?"

"I just know. From what you've told me about her, I just know. One pair of shoes has rhinestones all over the heels."

"And the colour of the bedroom walls?"

"I don't think that's important here. It's the cupboard that's important — all those fancy shoes."

"Where does she go in them?"

"That's up to you.")

When he told her that he was leaving, that he could not give up this girl, she asked him to give her a photograph of himself, the one that was used on the back cover of his first book. He wrote across it, "To my dear, dear friend. I'll always be there when you need me." She read it through her tears, then she thanked him for it and asked him to get out.

"I'll just pack a bag..."

"Now!" she said. "Just get out. Right now! You can come back tomorrow. I won't be here."

The next day, she was gone — with a trunk and anything that she felt was exclusively hers. (There wasn't much.) She wanted to bake bread, leave a meal of some sort — he had never really cooked in his life — show him how much she cared, how much he needed *her*. Instead, she left the photograph on the kitchen table.

("This is 1935-45? Is that right?"

"Right."

"He would have had stuffed animals everywhere. A stuffed pheasant, a deer's head over the mantlepiece, a squirrel. There is only one really comfortable chair and that is his — indisputedly his. Black leather, stuffed with horsehair, and the leather has begun to crack. Nobody else ever sits in that chair. There is a spinet piano, with some sheet music open on it, though no one ever plays the piano now that his wife is dead. The housekeeper mutters and complains as she dusts all this stuff, but he refuses to change anything or throw anything out. He has a large gold watch and the small boy is allowed to sit on his knee and hold it up to his ear."

Then Peter would go back to his study, humming.)

It was a strange hotel that they found. The town, at first, did not impress them, and they were about to turn around, when they saw a sign pointing down a small street, a cul de sac, really, near the post office. The hotel turned out to be right on the river and it had once been a small château. It was dripping in ivy and the small towers (one of which, they discovered with delight, contained the WC on their floor) were covered in shield-shaped slates, which overlapped one another, like fish scales. The patron turned out to be a patronne, very young, with short dark hair and a small son of about two years. Her husband was the chef and they had just, that week, taken over running the hotel. ("Which accounts," said Peter, later, "for the smell of burnt toast and the sense of incipient disaster.") On a whim of Peter's ("I may want to work the whole night through"), they decided to splurge and take two rooms, next to each other, on the third floor.

"Deux chambres?" The young Frenchwoman, who was no doubt as practical as she was beautiful, gave him a rather strange smile.

"Oui. Je suis écrivain. Quelques-fois, il est necessaire que je travaille tout le long de la nuit."

She shrugged. It was their money, after all.

So they took the car back to Perigueux and came down on the local train. Peter was very excited.

"It's a good place. The river. The isolation. And we can take walks, picnics. Oh!" he said, squeezing her hand and staring at the countryside with hungry eyes. "Here's where I'm going to break through the surface!" It was important for him to finish here. Then, he could write: "Lalinde, Perigord, May, 1979."

"Please, God," she thought, looking down at his long slim hand over hers (he had gorgeous hands, the hands of a musician; elegant, almost patrician), "please let it all come true."

"You won't be bored?" he said anxiously. "We haven't been to Lascaux."

"I won't be bored. And we'll save Lascaux for the next time. I

43

have a feeling that we'll be back."

"Yes. I feel it too. Strange, isn't it? As though we were meant to come here."

By the end of the first week, the yellow rose at their table had wilted and the petals had fallen off. Just the stem and a bit of fern stuck out of the tall thin pewter pitcher. Voices were often raised in the kitchen and dinner wasn't always on time. But it didn't matter—none of it mattered. There was the river and the town itself (artichokes growing in backyards, birdsongs, roses everywhere, an old woman who walked ahead of them one day, along a narrow street, rapping on windows. A woman's head would appear and a saucepan would be thrust out. The old woman would set the saucepan on the street and carefully pour out milk from a tin pail. The saucepan was handed back in, through the window, and a few francs were handed out. A boy on the bridge showed them a very large fish in a plastic bucket that he had caught and offered to lend them his pole. "Bonjour, M'sieu-Dame. Bonjour, M'sieu-Dame." The husband and wife clocks chimed the measured hours.)

And, back at the hotel, there was plenty to catch their interest. The young patronne treated them with a kind of amused contempt, but then, she treated everyone that way, including her husband and son. When Peter ordered an extra bottle of wine three nights running, she gave him an amused smile, and he said: "C'est un de nos pêches." She looked at him and laughed. "C'est un de nos pé-*chés*," she said abruptly. "Un de nos péchés." She wore the same green dress and navy blue cardigan all week. "She's a mystery, that one," Peter said. He concluded, because she did not respond to him (and most women did), that she had no sense of humour. "Harassed air, always, but really very competent. I wonder if the harassed air is put on." She fascinated him. Later, he speculated that she might be pregnant, or that she had married the chef, only because he could cook. The chef, a young man with sallow skin and a sweet smile, was rarely seen outside of the kitchen. Peter talked to him once or twice and found him rather boring, unworthy of such an interesting woman. The child looked just like his mother, with curly black hair and her translucent, exquisite skin. His name was Pierrot—

44

"le même nom que moi," Peter told him—and he liked to wander through the dining room, or around the terrace, watching the diners, receiving compliments on his good looks. Always, his mother came after him, with her harassed air, said something loud and mock-angry (the sort of public statement that mothers make when they know they are being overheard) and led him away. "There's a story here," Peter said. "It's difficult to stick with what I brought with me." At his request, she took a picture of him and the little boy sitting under one of the faded umbrellas.

("I love you," he wrote to her at the end of the year. "I can't help it. I just do." Her sister, her mother and her friends were horrified. "How can you be so *accommodating*?" they cried. "How can you still love that bastard?" She did not care what they said, and she did not despise herself for taking him back. She was not the same woman that she was when he left. She knew that she was the one who could survive, not he. And she knew in some terrible, deep, fundamental way that she owed it to him to take him back. She was not clever with words and could not have explained it, but she had done something to him over the years, had crippled him in some essential way, as surely as if she had cut off his toes with one of those wicked-looking knives that she saw here on market day. She saw her forgiveness as almost saint-like. For the first few nights, he wept in her arms. But she knew that she was no saint. One day, she actually had an image of herself behind him, pushing his chair around forever, his legs covered in a soft plaid robe. So that, when he flirted with his students or young girls in ticket booths, or with this beautiful young patronne, for instance, she no longer worried. He would never leave her again, or, if he did, he would soon return. And she—she would stay or not, as she chose. She made her "conditions" very clear. *She* was the strong one. My God, she was strong! That's what he had seen (but he had not seen that she had made him weak).

She heard the toilet flush in the WC next door, and she heard him go back to his room to wash and fetch his bottle. She had been kneeling on the windowseat for a long time and her legs were stiff. She washed in the sink that was hidden behind a pretty screen, and she thought about how much she was looking forward to dinner. It was like being on a ship, this holiday. She felt suspended in time, lazy, interested only in meals and conversation and the passing scene. It would be nice to stay away forever.

On the terrace, she sat across the table from him, her back to most of the other diners.

"They're having the 55," he said, as they waited for their soup. It was a game that they played when they went abroad.

"Who?"

"Les Anglais."

"How do you know?"

"They've just been handed the 'saw-mon few-may'."

"Do you think they are married?"

"No. She was probably hitchhiking and he picked her up. With the main course, he'll start telling her the story of his life."

("Et vous," said the old woman on the train, "do you have any children?" "No," she said, and then, she added, because it was expected of her, "Hélas.")

# TED'S WIFE

It was Phyllis Keeping who first called Ted's wife, "the alternate selection." It was at the Garwood's annual Christmas party. There was a lull in the conversation and Phyll, who seemed to be listening intently to something old Mrs. Garwood was saying, suddenly looked up and asked in a loud, clear voice (as though she'd been waiting to say it, thought more than one person, later): "Well, where's Ted, and, oh dear, what's her name? I always think of her as the alternate selection." No one actually gasped—Phyll was known for her wicked tongue—and one or two people laughed; but Anne Garwood, who had been busy passing around the hot hors d'oeuvres (the party was still thought of as Belle Garwood's Annual Do, although Anne and Jim really gave it, did all the preparations, and, for the last two years, opened their own home, rather than have Belle breathe in all that stale smoke the next day), said quietly and firmly ("Really," she thought to herself, "that woman is too much!"): "Ted and *Helen*," letting her voice underline the word, "are coming on the 6:15. I imagine that it's late."

"Helen!" cried Phyll, as though only just remembering it. "*Helen*. Of course!"

People went back to talking in little groups, admiring the Christmas tree, which, this year, had been decorated entirely

47

with things from the island: long chains of scarlet arbutus berries, shells, gilded pine cones. It really was pretty. ("Although you have to be one of the island Raj," Phyllis would say, the next day, "to get away with decorating your Christmas tree with clam shells. I was surprised that there wasn't a gilded starfish on the top.")

"Peace on earth, good will to men—which we must assume includes women too," Anne said to Jim, as they were cleaning up. "You'd think that woman would lay off, in honour of the season, if not out of some feeling for Ted. Of course, her remarks will be all over the island tomorrow."

"I doubt if Ted will hear it, or, if hearing, care."

"*She* may. Helen. Both hear it and care. I think Phyll Keeping gets more and more like some horrid character out of *Volpone*."

"She drinks too much at parties."

"She drinks too much all the time, but sometimes I think that the drinking is just a cover."

He shook his head at her, not quite sure what she meant. His mouth was full of the last of the smoked salmon.

"Well, if she drinks too much, she can always use that as an excuse for the kind of thing that she says. So can other people— and do. 'Oh, you know Phyll,' they say. I suspect that she's just naturally vicious and the drinking is really an excuse to be vicious in public and get away with it. When Ted and Helen finally did arrive, you saw what happened—how everyone stopped talking, except your mother, who hadn't caught Phyll's remark. That's the trouble with that kind of wit—it's far too clever—you don't forget what's been said. She would probably have been terrific in advertising."

"Putting down the other product."

"Yes, you're right. Well, she certainly has it in for Helen."

"That's understandable."

"She wanted Ted all to herself."

"To herself and Dave."

"'To herself and Dave,' yes. One tends to forget that Dave's involved in this. I'm always surprised that he puts up with her behaviour."

"Maybe she wasn't always this way."

"She certainly has never been quite so bad."

"Well, her remark says it all. It was clever, but not really apt, now, was it?"

"You mean, 'the alternate selection' to whom?"

"Exactly. People won't get it — most people. It will just stick in their minds in connection with Helen."

"But then, they'll start asking themselves what Phyll meant."

"And wonder if she — ?"

"Yes. And she, not being free —." He broke off. "Bloody woman. Let's go to bed. She's managed to be the centre of *our* attention for far too long."

It was a strange remark and people did comment on it. Most of Phyll's remarks were as obvious as they were witty — calling the fat couple who'd been staying with the Mackenzies, "Babar and Celeste," or the visiting minister, "Extreme Unction." You got that right away (or as soon as you'd seen the couple or talked to Reverend Manly for more than five minutes). But Ted had not run away from or divorced his wife; she had died, very suddenly, after a brief illness. And they had been devoted to one another. So, "the alternate selection" to whom? In the following weeks, there developed two schools of thought about this remark: one was that Phyll had unconsciously revealed that she and Ted had a "thing" for one another, but as she was married to Dave (and again, in a very happy marriage), she was not free to go to Ted when Mary died; the other was that the remark was *very* conscious and that it was precisely what Phyll wanted people, including Helen, to think.

Phyllis had been awfully helpful after Mary died and this seemed only natural at the time. The two couples had been friends for years and Dave and Ted worked in the same department, although in different fields. When Ted asked for a six-month leave of absence, so that he could go abroad and do some research, busy himself, so that he wouldn't brood after Mary's death, it was Dave and Phyllis who backed him up and urged him on, and Phyll, in particular (because she was on the island all the time), who promised to feed the cats and check in on his house every day. Phyll had even thrown a small farewell party at Madrona Inn and had given Ted a blank book in which to keep a journal. A whole bunch of them went down to see him off at the ferry the day that he left for London. Dave was driving him in, as Ted's car had been put up on blocks until his return. It had been a beautiful morning in early June and Ted seemed touched that so many people would get up at such an early hour (the ferry left at 8 a.m.) to wish him well. Phyll said later that she thought that he looked awfully frail, that he seemed to have aged terribly in the last three months. She wondered if going abroad and away from all his friends was such a good idea after all. On the island, she had made a special point of kissing both Ted and Dave as they came off the ferry on Friday nights during the term, and insisted on driving him back to his house (where the lights had already been put on and the refrigerator checked for ice). You could see her at the farmer's market on Fridays ("Well, we're all dressed like farmers at least," Phyll said once, laughing as she waited her turn, "although what I see in front of me is a poet; and in front of him, a renegade engineer; and in front of *him*, a superannuated hippie") buying a few extra goodies for Ted, along with her own weekend purchases. And she always invited him for at least one meal, even though she didn't see Dave from Monday to Friday and they always enjoyed their time alone together. When Ted protested about the loaves of fresh bread, the flowers on his bed-side table (for of course she had a key to his place and could come and go as she chose), she asked him what he thought friends were for? And it was she who helped him go through Mary's things, her only sister being 4,000 miles away, putting them in cardboard boxes and taking them in, depending upon their age and condition, to the Sally-Ann or the New-to-You shop in Victoria. Ted had been going to offer everything to the thrift shop on the island, until Phyll said, in horror, "Do you really want to see your wife's dresses coming at you along the road? Or her shoes on someone else's feet?" ("At which point, he looked at me blankly and said, 'Oh no, of course not,' and promptly burst into tears. I could've bitten off my tongue.")

Ted and Mary had been on the island longer than Dave and Phyll; indeed, it was an invitation to their friends' house on a crisp October weekend that made them fall in love with the place and eventually buy. That was when land was still relatively cheap, just before this particular island became one of *the* places to buy (Phyll called it "The Last Resort")—and they found a glorious acreage, right up above the Pass, that was an easy, pretty walk from Ted and Mary's. They kept their apartment in town, even after they renovated the old farmhouse on their property. Dave had ten more years until retirement, and Ted, five; both of the wives opted for living on the island more or less fulltime and the men arranged their schedules so that their teaching was fitted into four days, which gave them from Friday night until Monday night (sometimes even Tuesday morning) at home. The two men actually got on somewhat better than the two women. For one thing, Mary was much older than Phyll; and she was a painter. She had a small studio on the very edge of their property and she went there every weekday, rain or shine, when Ted wasn't home. She laughed at her paintings and called herself "the eternal amateur," but really, they were quite good, abstract without being blobs, and the colours were bold and brilliant, quite unlike what you would imagine a frail, rather conservative person like Mary would produce. She was beginning, finally, to have a "name," at least in British Columbia, when she dropped dead, literally, one Sunday evening. ("We were sitting around the fireplace, laughing at some silly story that Ted was relating, when Mary got up and said, 'Excuse me, but—' and fell over. She died before we were really out of our seats. Ted kept saying, 'Mary, Mary?' the way you do on a telephone when the line suddenly goes dead. Finally, the Hovercraft came and took them away—he, walking by the stretcher, still holding her dead hand; Dave, on the other side, holding him. I went back into the house and there was the fire, still crackling, and Mary's wine glass at the edge of the carpet where it had rolled, and a big wine stain that had spread like blood. I washed up and tidied the sitting room, and scrubbed the carpet as best I could, and then, I just sat there, wondering what it would be like to go like that, to feel suddenly strange—you know, she'd had a bad heart for years—and stand up, try to say something, and just be struck down, wham, your life slammed shut. I knew that Ted and Dave probably wouldn't be back until the morning, so I went home and went to bed and lay there, absolutely rigid with fear, the way I used to lie when I was a child so that 'THEY' wouldn't know that I was awake and come out of the corners and murder me. I imagined the most horrible scenes of Mary—who was so elegant, you know, and so private —being undressed and put on one of those tables, cut into, explored and examined like a piece of defective machinery, her heart held up to the light. By the time they returned on the regular ferry, the next morning, I was almost catatonic. And Ted—well! It was Dave who kept us all going through the next few days.")

But Phyll hadn't really known Mary all that well. The "age" thing and the "painting" thing (Mary wasn't interested in coffee mornings or the Golf Club), and a certain general reserve which she had, made it awfully difficult for Phyll to get through to her. It was not as though Mary were thorny, like a hedge of the wild roses that grew everywhere on the island, but rather, that she was distant. It was as though there were a long forest path between her and a woman like Phyll. And maybe the path was like one of those old logging trails, which led nowhere in the end, after you'd been stumbling along it for what seemed like hours. Despite this, Mary was more relaxed on the weekends, when Ted was there, and the four of them often ate together, or played silly games like Clue or Risk on long rainy Saturday evenings. Ted was reserved himself, but he was a wonderful storyteller and mimic. He had travelled quite a lot as a young man and could do killing imitations of border officials, policemen giving directions, lonely old ladies at English seaside resorts complaining about the soup. Phyll said once that he should have been an actor, not a scholar, and people still talk about his performance as Scrooge, some years before. Phyll pouted a little because there weren't any meaty women's parts in that dramatization and she nearly voted against it, but she was the first to rush up and kiss Ted and tell him how absolutely wonderful he had been. (But she got her own back when her Puck was praised in the island paper, *The Barnacle*, the next spring.)

Phyll's days were very busy. She had a huge successful vegetable garden, which everyone told her was like a painting or a tapestry, for she planned it for eye appeal as well as for nutrition.

She typed Dave's papers for him, and sometimes Ted's as well. And she did her share of volunteer work, driving old ladies and gentlemen to the outpatients' clinic in Victoria or on Salt Spring Island, driving the same people to the corner store or the farmers' market on Fridays. "Hither and yawn," as she sometimes called it. ("My God, how they do run on about food and ailments! I'm tempted sometimes to get earplugs. I hope when I get like that, they shoot me!")

She liked opera and went into the city regularly in the winter, meeting Dave on the mainland, for a change, and they would have a nice dinner, either before or after the opera, and perhaps see friends. Sometimes, they made up a foursome with Ted and Mary and they went to see a play.

"People ask me what I *do* over here," Phyll would complain laughingly to weekend guests. "To me, there never seems to be enough hours in the day." They would marvel at her big wood-stove, on which she had just cooked a wonderful meal, and they would get up the next day to breakfast on her homemade bread and jam and freshly ground coffee. She would show them where to empty the compost bucket and take them on nature walks. She saw to it that they returned to the mainland dazzled. (Although, sometimes, she complained to Dave that she wondered if they were running a convalescent home. At which point, he would laugh and say, "Well, don't do it then," knowing full well that she thrived on it. "What a Queen you are, Phyll," he said to her once. She was quite annoyed. "I don't feel much like a queen when I'm emptying all those ashtrays or running the last of the guests' sheets through the washing machine." "Oh yes, you do," he said. "You feel more like a queen than ever — a queen in exile. One of those royal persons who would be a queen if the monarchy hadn't been overthrown." "I don't think that you're very nice," she said, really hurt by his remarks. "Most of them are *your* friends or *your* students, after all." But he simply picked up the garbage can with a smile and said, "But *your* invitations," and he went outside.

After Ted went away on leave, she discovered that she missed him far more than she missed Mary, but she would never have told anyone that — not even Dave. She had always had a suspicion that Dave was just a tiny bit jealous of her friendship and rapport with Ted—they got on so well and so easily together. Mary was ten years older than Ted and she coddled him to such a degree—or so it seemed to Phyll—that Phyll admitted that she'd been shocked to discover some beautiful nightdresses ("Real silk, my dear, and dripping in lace. The kind of thing that you're given, not the kind of thing that you buy.") among Mary's clothes. She never before thought of their relationship as sexual. ("I felt as though I'd caught him sleeping with his mother!") Now, she imagined how Ted would make love—with great gentleness and wit, she thought. She envied Mary those nightgowns, for they could only have come from Ted. But with her bad heart? Had he ever been able to let himself go? Wouldn't he always have to be thinking of her, of whether or not he was too heavy on her, or if he were asking too much? (But he was actually very tall and thin—he would probably hardly be any weight at all.) What did he do now that Mary was dead? Did he miss her *physically*? (She had been cremated; there was no gravestone.) But she must have been over seventy! How often would a seventy-year-old woman want to make love, especially if her heart were bad? Phyll took away the nightgowns and burnt them. It would be wrong for anyone else to wear them.

At first, Ted had written regularly—at least once a week. He rented a flat in London and was doing some work at the British Museum, something to do with *Beowulf* and the Sutton Hoo Ship Burial. The letters came to Dave, of course, as was only proper, but they were addressed to them both inside, "Dear Dave and Phyll," and she was sure that a lot of the descriptions of people and places were for her benefit. He was having some trouble sleeping, he said, and he had taken to getting up very early and going for long walks, when all the rest of the city was asleep. He stood on Westminster Bridge at 5 a.m., waiting for Big Ben to strike. He walked to the new Covent Garden at Vauxhall and loved all the vegetables and flowers, as gorgeous as ever, but missed "the noise and disorder and confusion of the old." He described the warnings, everywhere, about unattended parcels, and the "Arabs running around Harrod's in their white nighties." "And the famous London taxicab is no longer as black and uniform as the businessman's umbrella. I have seen maroon cabs, blue ones, even a white cab! But just when I think London —never mind London Bridge—is falling down, falling down, I see a sign from the top of a bus on Regent Street. I suppose that I think of it now because it was a shop that specialized in those wonderful black umbrellas. Running around the top of the windows, in discreet gold lettering on black, the store announced that it also sold 'life preservers, sword canes and dagger cases.' The Empire is not dead yet (at least on Regent Street)." He enclosed, however, a Bird's custard label with the instructions in English, French and Arabic.

"Bird's custard!" Phyll said. "Whatever is that poor man eating?" She began to think about the kind of meals that she would prepare for him when he returned. Thick fish chowders and pot roasts that were marinated in wine. Grilled salmon. *Crisp* vegetables. Blackberry-and-apple pies. She imagined herself down on the dock meeting him, in the new wine-coloured cardigan that she was knitting (somehow Dave was never there with them). She copied out a line of *Beowulf* and memorized it: Wæs þu, Hrothgar, hal!" She could see his face light up with happiness. And back at the house, waiting, she would have hot apple juice and rum, and some of her famous fruitcake. He had promised that he would return before Christmas and that he would spend the holidays with them.

At the end of October, he suddenly decided to go to Greece. "I know I won't get a 'beaker of the warm south' at this time of the year—half a glass, if I'm lucky—but my work here is nearly done, and looking at the Elgin Marbles the other day, I suddenly had a great longing, since I'm more than halfway there, to see the Parthenon at sunset. It was something Mary and I always intended to do, but we never got around to it. Maybe I want to see it for her as well, who knows? Anyway, I'm off tomorrow, just like that, leaving all my academic paraphernalia with my landlady, who shakes her head over the whole business ('And 'im, such a proper gentleman too!'), but who has promised to keep it in her box-room until I pick it all up on the way home."

Phyll thought that for all the lightness of the tone, he sounded very melancholy, maybe suicidal, although Dave couldn't see how she was getting that out of the letter at all.

"Well, I just *feel* it, the reference to Mary and sunsets and rushing off so suddenly."

"I think that it sounds very healthy myself."

"You think that everyone's healthy unless they're actually broken open and bleeding. *I* think that he's very lonely and unhappy. I'm even toying with the idea of flying out to join him for a week or so."

Dave looked at her. "Leave him alone. He knows what he's doing." (But, what Dave didn't know, what she had never told him — or anyone, in fact — was that, when Ted had broken down that afternoon over Mary's clothes and shoes, she had reached out her arms to him and had rocked him against her, as he wept, saying over and over again, "Oh my dear, my dear." Something had passed between them that day, something very rare and very fine; their friendship had entered a new and deeper stage. It would never be spoken of or acted upon unless Dave — . But that was silly; they loved each other very much. And besides, he was as strong as an ox.)

She didn't go, of course. That would have been too risky all round. But she did fret about him and wrote him even longer, wittier letters than ever before, one a day on the days that Dave wasn't there, usually late in the afternoon when she had just come in from her walk and her cheeks were still damp and alive from the wind and the sea air. She would build up the fire, get out the sherry and begin. "Time spent with you," she wrote him in one letter, "it makes me feel very close. Is the Greek light all that it's cracked up to be?"

He found rooms, after a week, in a kind of pension in what had been the old Turkish quarter, "with the Hill of the Muses and Philopappou just above me. I climb there every day, just before sunset, lean against the monument, and look across at the Acropolis. As the wonderful honey-coloured light flows down, I forget all about the pollution, the incessant noise of the automobiles, the horrible lumps of grilled meat that are cooking in the over-priced tavernas — all the crass commercialism of this city. It's erased in an instant and I come as close to a mystical experience as I'm ever likely to get."

The weather, surprisingly, held. And in the *Pension Olympia,* "congenial strangers" came and went. "I feel that I'm beginning to re-cover or un-cover, or something, and I even wish that I'd become a classical scholar, instead of immersing myself in the cold northern waters of Early English." He began to talk of a trip, to Delphi, Meteora and Thessalonika, that he was planning to take "with one or two others." After that, it was only post-cards ("Don't worry, I'm keeping a journal and taking pictures, you shall see and hear it all later") until, one day, in late November, Dave brought over an air-letter which said that he would be arriving, as planned, in a couple of weeks, and that he would phone them from the airport. "Don't bother to meet me. There are one or two things I must do in town, and, by the way, I shall be bringing someone with me." It was a typical November night and the rain drummed against the roof and hurled itself at the window panes. Any minute now, they'd have a power failure. Phyllis willed herself to sit still on the couch and sip at her drink while Dave read the letter aloud, as was his custom. When he finished, he handed the letter to her with a smile.

"I wonder who 'someone' is?" she said, trying to keep her voice steady. "'Stoke the fire and kill the fatted calf.' It must be someone special. I never thought of Ted as sly before."

"How about shy, instead of sly? Maybe he's fallen in love."

"At his age? He's an old man!" She poured herself another drink.

"Not really, and even if he is—in the eyes of this youth-oriented culture anyway—what would it matter? He sounds happy. Aren't you happy for him?"

"Oh yes, of course." She was terrified that she was going to burst into tears at any minute. Who? Who? How dare.... "Only if he were happy and it was all right wouldn't he write reams and reams about it, the way all lovers do? No," she said, "there's something strange, when 'someone' doesn't even have a name." She poked at the fire and smiled. "Unless...."

"Unless what? What are you grinning at?"

"Unless 'someone's' name would indicate that she's a he."

Phyllis had long since ceased to shock him. Or so he thought. "That's ridiculous!"

"Is it? *Is* it? He always seems to have a following of earnest young men. And he was a confirmed bachelor until he was well over thirty. Then, he married an older woman." (Mentally, she rearranged the evidence of the nightgowns. Not gifts from a lover consumed with passionate intensity, but desperate purchases by a middle-aged woman yearning to be held and entered.)

Dave laughed.

"We all have followings of earnest young men. Earnest young women too. That's part of the whole mystique. Ted may have more men than women, simply because his field seems to attract more men than women."

"Why?"

"Why? I don't know why. Perhaps because you get a lot of pedants in Early English—or used to. It's all changing."

Phyllis smiled again. "Do I make up one bed or two, I wonder?" The three of them sitting around a log fire had become four, one of them a handsome young Greek of about twenty-seven, a poet perhaps. His white teeth gleamed, as he smilingly struggled to follow the conversation. This was a picture, a re-arrangement that she could accept. So long as she did not dwell on what the two of them did when they were alone. She accepted that kind of thing, of course, but she didn't really like to think about men—about Ted and his Greek friend—fucking each other in the ass.

"Listen," Dave said. "Don't go around speculating aloud, will you?"

"About what?"

"You know, 'about what.' About Ted coming back with a man."

"Ah ha! So you think I might be right?"

"I don't know. You have an awful way of getting to the heart of the matter. But, I think that, in fairness to Ted, you might keep your thoughts to yourself."

"Do you think that he would be ostracized? People on this island are pretty sophisticated, you know."

"No.... I don't know. People on this island—your crowd, anyway—pretend to be sophisticated. I think that they are actually conservative."

58

"Oh, very well. My lips are sealed. But I bet I'm right!"

And at first glance, it looked as if she *were* right. The night that Ted arrived was dark and stormy, and the ferry was late getting in. They didn't see him in the first rush of foot passengers and they were wondering whether or not he'd missed the boat after all, when Dave shouted, "There he is!" and began to wave.

"Look at 'someone,'" Phyll said triumphantly, "he looks positively delicious."

"Look again," Dave said, laughing. "I hate to spoil your fantasy, Phyll, but look again."

And it wasn't a boy. It was definitely a girl, a young woman, with her hair tucked up in a knitted cap, who was holding onto Ted's gloved hand, and pulling behind them one of those wheelie-carts that was piled high with luggage. Dave rushed forward to help them, but Phyllis just stood there, while men, women, children and dogs hurried past her, up the wharf. Her heart was beating so fast and so hard that she was sure that everyone could hear it. She thought of the chaste bed that she'd made up in Ted's spare room. How they would laugh about that! She thought of how hard she'd worked the past few days to make the place sparkle and shine; she thought of the loaf of sourdough rye that she put on the kitchen table, the jar of her apple butter beside it and the bottle of Ouzo chilling in the fridge. She thought of the special trip that she'd taken to Victoria to get *that,* and to look up the words, "welcome home," in Greek at the public library. And the present under his pillow, with the note saying, "My dear, now I will feel complete again." The note was the worst thing of all.

And, the shock of it all, the rage—and what a fool he'd turned out to be. So that, when Ted and Helen gave a *Twelfth Night* party, and Ted, at the end of the feasting, tapped on his wine glass and said, shyly, "Well, we've decided to make it legal," Phyll's voice, drunken, but high and hard and clear, cut across the congratulations and applause with her best line yet.

"What are you going to do," she cried, "adopt her?"

## HARRY AND VIOLET

He had been sulky all day—like the summer weather back East, she thought, when you looked at the sky and brought in the garden chairs, rolled up the windows on the car. It was understandable. Now, he was going to have to share her. There were hours to go before the ferry arrived, and yet, already, she could feel herself being pulled in two directions.

"Come for a swim?" he said.

"No thanks, I have—" (no, don't do that, be honest) "I *want* to clean out her room."

"Couldn't you do that later?"

"Yes, but I'd rather finish all the dirty work before I go swimming, not after."

So he went down the path, towel over his shoulders, whistling loudly, without her. "Men," she thought, tipping the dustpan into the wood stove, and then, she stopped still, remembering him sitting up in bed this morning, teasing her, smiling. "I love him," she thought, and then, "Goddammit" and then (with a sigh), "Well, there's no law that says *they* have to love one another." Later, when she ran down to the store for some marshmallows—they'd have a wiener roast tomorrow, maybe drive to the park at the south end of the island, make it a real treat; the child liked it down there, because there were old logs that she could ride on, like horses, out into the bay—she saw him over on the rocks, sitting with his hands around his knees, thinking. She waved, but he didn't see her.

"Oh well," she thought, "let him sulk." (But she went back up the path discouraged.)

There were fresh sheets on the child's bed and a posy of wildflowers in a green bottle on the dresser. Also, a little tin candlestick that she herself had used, twenty-five years before, at her grandfather's summer place. She could still read the faded lettering:

*Jack be Nimble*
*Jack be Quick*

There had been no electricity, at first, at her grandfather's place, and her mother would accompany her, carrying the candlestick, into the back room where she slept. It was one of the few things from her childhood that she still owned, that candlestick. Now, she regretted lost teddybears, a certain little tea set and a doll with a china head named Miss Nanoo. She would like to have given all those things to her little girl. And the little whistling tea kettle, a pop-up book about a family named the Jolly Jump-Ups; all the high-heeled shoes, and hats with polka-dot veils, for playing ladies. (But not the rabbits that died, or the stairs that creaked, or her parents' low-pitched furious arguments coming up the hot-air registers.)

"Sometimes, in town, I feel like I ought to make an appointment to see you," he said, "in order to get any real, undivided attention. Maybe that's what—"

"What's what?" she asked, sitting up.

"Nothing," he said, and pulled her down again. "Nothing." He had such beautiful skin; she loved to run her hands down his long back and over his buttocks.

"I'll bet that you were a really naughty little boy," she said indulgently. "I'll bet that your mother had a lot of trouble with you."

"With all of us."

"With you, especially."

He laughed and rolled over on his back. "I guess so." He imitated a mother's voice. "You get into that house right now or I'll really give you something to cry about."

"God," she said, "I bet that I sound like that sometimes. I hear women in supermarkets or on the street and I wish they could hear themselves—so angry and irritated."

"No, you don't sound like that. You're far too soft with that kid. That's what's wrong with her."

"She's had a hard time; she's very insecure."

"I think that you make it harder."

"How?" she said. "How?" Sitting up again. "I do the best that I can."

"Listen, that kid runs you. She's fucking spoiled, that's what she is."

"You don't like kids."

"That's not true."

"It is true and you know it."

Where had their closeness gone? Lying in her secret sunbathing place, beyond the apple trees, tasting each other, touching, exploring. Now, it was as if the sun had suddenly disappeared behind a cloud.

But most of the time, it had been lovely—just the two of them, for a change. "Our honeymoon," she said to him, laughing. They got up late and had special breakfasts on the porch, talking and drinking coffee, and watching the boats in the channel. Once, a big freighter went by and they spent a while daydreaming out loud and saying to each other, "Let's chuck it all and the three of us just go away some place. A hut on a beach in Pago Pago. Breadfruit and pineapples. No need for clothes or cars. Climb up and pick your breakfast; swim out and spear your dinner. Ah yes." The freighter seemed enormous in the narrow channel; the sound of its engines throbbed long after the boat disappeared. Her eyes weren't good enough, but he made out the name: "Tana Maru. Oh well, Japan! Why not?"

"We could fly dragon kites and live in a paper house."

"How could we make love in a paper house?"

"Quietly," she said.

"Not you," and laughed when she blushed.

63

"Anyway," she said, "freighters don't take children under twelve."

"How do you know?"

"Oh, I know. I know. It's one of my big fantasies. I've got a book. What do you want to know? 'Best Buys in Freighters to the South Seas and Australia'? 'To the Orient, Far East, West-bound from Pacific Coast Ports'? 'Best Buys in Freighters Between Japan and Australia'? They don't recommend container vessels."

"You really have a book?"

"Sure. I ordered it once, when I was feeling low. Something to dream about."

He told her about his first day in Paris, walking clear across the city and hardly stopping, all day long, drunk on the beauty and romance, feeling Europe soak in through his feet. Getting stuck with his backpack in a *pissoir*. He had been with his wife in Paris. They had walked the city together. She imagined them finding a small, perfect room on a sidestreet, making love behind wooden shutters, laughing at their swollen feet.

"It *would* be fun to go away," he said, "just the two of us."

"How can he be expected to understand?" she thought. "What does he really know about it?" *They* hadn't wanted children, he and his wife, or so *he* said.

"I can't understand why you're attracted to me," she said. She said it often.

"Because you're you."

And yet, he got upset, in town, if she couldn't drop everything and come for a walk, right then. He went by himself with his old black umbrella—a solitary figure in the rain. Sometimes, her heart ached for him, really ached, like a sore tooth, an ache that never completely went away. And yet, at other times, infuriated because he would not, *could* not understand, she saw his ego as a very large dog, which he took with him everywhere and which expected to be constantly fed. A Saint Bernard of an ego. No. Something a little more vicious, a German shepherd perhaps.

"Why are you attracted to me?" he said. He said it often. "What is it about me that attracts you?"

And she would list all the things that she loved about him—and the list was long—as they sat over their wine in the June twilight. It was a sort of game between them.

They fought too—they both had terrible tempers. But here, there hadn't been any small worried voice to suddenly pipe in with, "Hey, are you guys having a fight?"

Sunday mornings, for example. Sunday mornings had always been her special time. Particularly over here, on holiday, but also, somewhat modified, in town. She liked to lie in bed, with a book and a pot of coffee. He wanted to make love, and then, be up and doing, have a half-decent breakfast, not just sixteen cups of coffee. "Well," he would say, rolling over, "I don't know about you, but I'm getting hungry." It was hard. She found herself reading the same page two or three times. But she forced herself to look at him sweetly, from over the top of the book, and turn the page. He was not used to such treatment; he was hurt and angered by it. She was no longer used to sharing her Sunday mornings with a man. (And, of course, to make matters worse, it was the morning that the child was allowed in bed, allowed a special cup of coffee and to bring a book.)

"But here in the cabin?" he remonstrated. "Look what a lovely day it is!" It was hard, but she would not give in. Could not. And yet, she could almost hear her mother's voice, haranguing her: "You let one get away! This one, too?" As though they were a fish or some big game animal.

"We have to learn to take each other as we are," she said, fighting an urge to get up and make him a cheese omelette, with some of the fresh parsley from under the shed, buttered toast and crisp bacon, a new pot of steaming coffee.

"It seems to me that what you really mean is that you won't change, that I have to do all the changing."

"No," she said, "that's not what I mean at all."

Or was it? He had two shirts that he couldn't wear any more because so many buttons had come off. What was she trying to prove? Was she really just a bitch? She had insisted that he learn to cook and share the cooking.

He liked things spare and neat and organized. She covered surfaces with a clutter of books and papers and jugs of flowers.

Pictures drawn by her little girl. Old things from secondhand stores. In her bedroom (their bedroom now), she had a large framed sepia photograph of a nurses' graduating class, in old-fashioned uniforms.

"Is one of those your grandmother?" he said, bending his head close to the picture, searching for a family likeness.

"Oh no," she said. "I saw it in a secondhand shop and thought that it was nice. On the back, it says 'Grace Harriett, 1916, second row from left in the back row.' See, that's her."

"You're nuts," he said. "You know that, don't you? Absolutely bananas."

But she refused to take the photograph down. She gave him one of the two bureaus and found herself doing it grudgingly. She admitted it, embarrassed and ashamed. The sight of his wallet and keys and loose change on the old bureau that she had so bravely painted a bright defiant red, the tears rolling down her cheeks (after changing the colour of the walls, changing the bedroom, actually, and even the side of the bed that she slept on)—it irritated her.

"You don't really want me in your life," he said.

"Oh, that's not it!" She went to him and put her arms around him. "I guess that I've learned my lesson a little *too* well. Give me time to get used to you. I haven't had a room of my own in ten years. I hated it at first, and then—and then I liked it. I'm sorry, I know that it's a little silly, but I wish we had space for separate bedrooms."

"And sleep separately? I can move out, you know. Maybe that would be the answer."

"*Not* sleep separately," she said. "Or only sometimes. I've got used to my own private space, that's all."

And he repeated again, "You just don't want me in your life."

He put a stop to the child crawling in bed with her. He wouldn't hear of it.

"She's jealous; she needs to know that she's wanted."

"This is our *bedroom*. She's not wanted in our bedroom. This is our *bed.* " Then he added, sulking, "It's you she wants to crawl in bed with anyway, not me."

"She needs to feel that I still love her. She needs cuddles, just as much as you and I do."

"What am I supposed to do, shove over?"

"Would that be so hard?"

"I'd have to start wearing underpants."

She began to laugh, and although he smiled, she could see that his mind was made up.

"Sometimes," he said, "I think that I can really understand why Tom left."

"How do you know that he felt the way you do? She's his child, after all."

"Yes, she makes that abundantly clear."

So, there they were again. Stalemate. She took to going down and crawling in with the child.


Sometimes, they asked each other if maybe it was only the sex.

"Our adult lives have been so different," she said. "You are used to so much personal freedom. I've never actually lived alone with a man for more than a few months. Maybe I like children because I've had to like them, who knows? But I do like them and I *love* my child—I *love* her. She's part of me, part of my life. She and I help each other grow."

"You're ruining her," he said.

She repeated, "What do you know about it?"

One winter, he and his wife had packed up and gone to North Africa. One winter, they had lived in a small cabin in Québec. They walked all night with a lantern, bundled up against the cold, running and laughing and making angels in the snow. They had been across the whole length of the country, stopping when it took their fancy, hitchhiking, delivering drive-away cars, washing dishes in resort hotels.

(Walking all day in the streets of Paris, their arms around each other.)

Sometimes, she wondered why, after all, he left. He never spoke against his wife; indeed, he loved her still and often saw her.

"She asked me if I was happy?" he said one night, weeping, with her arms around him tight.

67

"What did you say?" she whispered.

"I told her that happiness wasn't the point."

Oh, how she loved him for his honesty, even when his words flew into her like arrows! He buried his face in her neck.

"I love you," she whispered, her mouth against his cheek. "I love you. It's going to be all right." She saw his wife lying alone and weeping. His ex-wife. His X.

His car was clean and tidy. Nothing out of place. Hers contained old ferry tickets, the rubber leg off a doll, a scarf that somebody left behind a year ago and might return to claim, an empty apple juice carton, a brown glove left over from last winter.

"Why do we go on with this?" they sometimes cried to one another. "It's ridiculous!"

But the last four days had been, if not paradise, something very close to it. The weather held and they lay naked in the sun.

"We are each other's Africas," he said. "We need so much time and privacy to even begin to explore."

"I feel weightless," she said. "Like an astronaut." And she stuck an early rose behind her ear.

They sat on the wharf and watched the extravagant sunsets, then they came back up the path into the cool and private darkness. They fell deep into one another's secret places, and then, lay on the big double bed, their arms around one another, while the moon stared at their silvered bodies, with its single silver eye.

Once, they woke up and they both admitted that they had to pee, so they went outside together, still naked, into the soft June night, laughing. Everything simple and easy and understood between them. No secrets. (And no little voice to say, "Hey, what are you guys doing?")

"We shouldn't really sleep with the moonlight on us," she said. "It could drive us crazy."

"Impossible, in your case," he said, kissing her. But she stayed awake a long time after that, propped on her elbow, watching his dark head on the pillow.

The child called him Harry to tease him. Because of all his dark hair and dark rabbinical beard. She had a doll named Harry as well, a girl doll with a mop of red wool hair. She wondered if they would have been friends, the man and the child, in some other situation. It was she who came between them. They both wanted to possess her. No. Each wanted her to say that each was number one. What did *she* want? Both of them, but not so much pulling and tugging. And, if it ever came to a choice, there was none. Always, the child was first. In that, at least, he was right.

"It's easier without a man," she thought. "But is it better?" So many broken marriages and separated children. Now, her ex-husband was with a woman who didn't want any children—or not yet. They had been to Mexico and Guatemala. Driving. Stopping wherever it took their fancy. Postcards of beaches along the Oregon coast, Sausalito, Aztec ruins, the balloon sellers in Chapultepec Park in Mexico City. They brought back a *piñata* and lovely clothes for her and her daughter. A papier-mâché bird. A wooden children's game. An armload of paper flowers. The child was with them now. In a few hours, they would put her on the ferry with some friends who were coming across. They never came when she was here, and yet, her husband's presence was all around her. His old plaid shirt hung on a hook by the door. Even his pipe lay on the mantlepiece.

As she rolled out the pastry for a pie, she wondered how her—what? lover? new old man? boyfriend?—was affected by being surrounded by so much of her past. It was her house, her cabin—or hers and her ex-husband's. He owned half of a second-hand Volkswagen, his typewriter, his books, his knapsack and tent, a few clothes. He liked it that way, he said. It was easier to move about.

She had enjoyed these four days. Loved them. Wanted more. And yet she looked forward eagerly to the coming of the child, who reached some deep place in her, where no man could ever go, a place that could never be entered by any man, not even the father, no matter how much she had loved him.

Still, she wished that the solitary man on the rocks would come up the path right now and take her, floury hands and all, and lay her down on the big bed in the other room. And no need

69

to keep quiet. No ears to listen. Letting go.

She opened a jar of blackberry and apple and spooned it into the pie shell. "He wants me to come and get him," she thought. "I want him to come and get me."

She had not realized how lonely she was; indeed, that she was lonely at all, until she fell in love with him. When he first met her, he had not known about her child. She was alone in a café. They were reading the same book, only different volumes. Sometimes, she wondered if he felt that he had been led into her world under false pretences. The way one person will stand by the road — usually the woman — and stick out her thumb. Then, after the driver stops and is agreeable, she signals to her friend behind the bushes. What can the driver do? But it was not that she deliberately set out to deceive him, nothing like that. There they were in the café, reading the same book. Who noticed first? Who spoke first? They debated this sometimes. Talking and talking and talking. And then, they walked down to the beach and sat on a log and talked some more.

So that, by the time she said that she really had to go home now, she knew that he had never broken a bone in his life, that he liked Yeats and Bukowski, but not Eliot, that he had come for the very first time that afternoon to that café, that he was married and had no children. She mentioned the child, she must have. She always mentioned the child. But there she'd been, in a café, reading a book by herself, free to spend the afternoon sitting on a log and talking to a stranger. How was he to know that it was her one free afternoon a week? How was he to know what she meant when she said, "*I* have a child, a little girl." How was she to know that this stranger would fall in love with her?

They were both verbalizers. They turned their relationship (and everything else) over and over, looking for cracks, or even incipient cracks, giving little taps to test for clarity or weakness. (Only some things were never said, of course. How tall he was compared to.... How round she was compared to.... Being consciously careful, at first, to make no comparisons at all.) Laughing, then, at each other's irritating mannerisms. He sighed and groaned a lot; it did not mean that he was unhappy, he said, it was simply a habit. She snored if she slept on her left side. "Just wake me or turn me over if it bothers you."

He had been in the city before, five years ago, in the West End. They might have met then. Would they have liked one another? They spent whole afternoons trying to trace where each had been on some particular day.

After their second meeting, they knew that they must never see each other, alone, again.

He told her that sometimes he felt very lonely when he was with her, especially when he visited her in the communal house where she was living, even late at night, in the privacy of her own little bedroom (*her* bedroom). He felt the other people in the house; felt her ready to swing instantly from lover to mother at the sound of a distant cry.

"What would you have me do?" she said. "There are some things that I can't change."

"There are some things that you *won't* change."

"Perhaps. I don't know."

"I know it."

Often, they admitted that they weren't suited to one another. They laughed about it painfully—or cried. "Like two prisoners on a chain gang," she thought. "One tall; one short, whom Fate has manacled together."

The child was rude to him. "Why does he put ketchup on his eggs?" she said, the three of them sitting at the breakfast table. "Why does he, Mommy?"

"Ask him."

"She always turns to *you* to find out about *me*," he said.

"That's natural."

"She's rude."

And it was true. She was rude—at least to him. One day, she asked, "If you and Harry had a big fight, could you tell him to get out?"

"No," she said, "not really. He lives here now."

"But it's *your* house," said the little girl.

71

Sometimes she felt such anger towards that other man, the child's father, who had put her in this position. Sometimes she thought that the whole thing really wasn't worth the trouble. She had been happy that afternoon in the little café, reading her book, sipping her tea, enjoying her solitude. She hadn't been looking for anyone. All that sort of thing was behind her. He noticed her when she came in, he said, because, wherever he went, he always sat so that he could look at people. Had *he* been looking for someone? Had the business of the books seemed, to him, somehow a password? She had been tired that day—there were questions of mortgages and plumbing, a pregnant cat. She was waiting her turn to spend a weekend in the country. Yet, she saw this man who was reading the same book as she was. How long had he been watching her? Who smiled first? Who spoke? Later, he quoted Balthazar, when he asked if they could meet again: "'And morality is nothing if it is merely a form of good behaviour.'"

And she replied (Pursewarden): "'I know that the key I am trying to turn is in myself.'"


And now, here she was, making pies and putting lavender between the sheets. And a special pile of secondhand comic books, a miniature of the expensive, utterly worthless, but much-coveted cornflakes, so the little girl would have an easy and special breakfast in the morning, and not come in to wake her mother early. Or try to crawl in bed and be rebuffed. ("This is her first time over here with *you*," she cried to the invisible figure on the rocks. "She was allowed to do it! Right or wrong, she was allowed to do it. You're the adult, why can't you give a little?" But, why should he really? It was not his problem.)


After supper, they sat on the porch together, talking but not talking, really listening for the first cars as they came up from the ferry at the other end of the island.

"Already, it's not the same," he said. "I can feel it."

"I know." She put her small hand on top of his large one. "I've enjoyed these past four days. I've loved them. I guess that they seemed quite ordinary to you. I guess that this is the way you've always lived."

"Yes," he said. "With a woman, it's more or less the way that I've always lived. I'm not used to any other way."

"I love you," she said.

"In your way."

He let her go down the path alone when they heard the car stop. She was always surprised when her child had been away for a few days. How big she was! How badly her long hair needed cutting!

"Hello," she said, holding the child's face against her. "We've been waiting for you."

"I want to go and see if Connie's up," the child said. "I want to play with her tomorrow."

They went hand in hand across the road to her friend's house and arranged a picnic. The mother began to relax. Maybe it was she who caused the tension? The child wasn't going to be with them all the time; didn't want to be, in fact. She had been looking forward to seeing Connie, not them. What was she worrying about? Crossing the road again, they noticed a nest of tent caterpillars, just visible in the growing darkness.

"Can I have some, Mommy? Can I have some of those caterpillars in a jar?"

"Tomorrow," she said. "I'll fix you a jar with some holes in the lid for air."

"I'll just get two," the child said, giving a little skip. "I'm gonna name them Harry and Violet."

"We'll get them tomorrow," she promised.

(And who was Violet? It must be somebody over there. She realized with a start that her child had a whole other world "over there," that there were things which she wasn't told about, friends even. "And what do *they* do," she wondered, "about the crawling into bed?")

The child was tired and went to bed quite readily. She acknowledged the man's hug, even if she didn't exactly return it.

73

And she called him by his right name for a change. Her mother relaxed even more. It would work out. Perhaps all three of them had been too impatient, too hostile to the idea of change. The man and woman went back out on the porch for a while, just enjoying the night and the quiet, and then, they, too, went inside to sleep. They lay in the big bed with their arms around each other.

And they woke early, smiling, as they heard the child tiptoeing around the kitchen, fixing her special breakfast, as she'd been told to do. Important. Respectful of them, yet anxious to get going. Her mother fought down the impulse to run out and give her a good morning kiss. She was proud of her daughter, opening and closing the refrigerator door so quietly, rummaging in the cupboard so carefully. (What had been forgotten? Would she remember about the mousetraps? Again, the urge to run out and take her in her arms, pin her unruly hair out of her eyes, make sure she had a cardigan.)

But she made herself lie still, smiling into the eyes of the man, feeling him move close to her, feeling him stiffen against her naked thigh. She smiled when she heard the door of the cabin close.

"Come here you," he whispered, his eyes dark, his body hard and smooth against hers. "Come here."

She shook her head and pulled him over on top of her, felt him filling up all the empty spaces, clung to him, opened to him. She shut her eyes and with a great, almost child-like sigh, gave herself up to the lovely, wet, slippery union between them. Oh God, yes, she needed this too, and from this man who loved her, heaven alone knew why. She felt all the empty and sore places fill up, expand, smooth out. Oh God, it was so nice with his dark head in the hollow of her shoulder, the songbirds outside, she couldn't stand it much longer, and neither, she knew, could he. They were always urgent in the morning. Why? She could tell that he was coming and it excited her terribly, something about the way he—

"Harder," she whispered, "harder."

And the child said, from the foot of the bed,

"Hey, you guys, d'you want to meet Harry and Violet?"

# IN THE BLEAK MID-WINTER

Very early on, it had been established that Maggie was the frail one who needed just that extra bit of consideration and looking after. She had never been out of Canada before, except to England and Scotland, which didn't really count, did it? And she wasn't good with languages, didn't pick up basic words and phrases quickly and easily like the other two. And the Greek food disagreed with her, although she loved it. Tonight she had said that she was beginning to feel as if she had a Greek soul in a North American body! It was the heavy olive oil that really did her in and sent her running to the nearest *tooaléta*. Yet still she ordered Greek salad every night and put away the olives as though they were cocktail peanuts. When Patrick teased her about it, she defended herself on the grounds that eventually she would become immune to whatever it was in the oil that was causing her distress. She also reminded him that she had always had a weak stomach and he nodded, admitting that it was true. They told Johanna stories of amusing incidents involving Maggie's weak stomach and frantic searches for toilets or bushes when they had travelled across England and Scotland together.

Johanna smiled politely and looked at the menu. It seemed to her that Maggie was always reminding Patrick of their shared past. Johanna had not yet made up her mind whether Maggie was extremely simple or extremely clever. Whichever it was, she reflected, they always seemed to end up doing pretty much what Maggie wanted. Although it didn't seem that way; it seemed as though she, Johanna, and Patrick, were the strong ones. Maggie admired Johanna's facility with maps and waiters. Maggie would walk two miles in the wrong direction, she said, before she'd get up the nerve to ask the way.

And the men — the Greek men scared her half to death. Johanna didn't like the men either, the Athenians anyway. She didn't like the way they made remarks or pushed themselves up against you in the crowded yellow trams. But she wasn't afraid of them; they simply made her mad. She had travelled a lot on her own and she knew how to look a little to the left or right, never directly at them, never directly into their eyes; and she had, in the course of her travels, learned how to say in several languages (Greek being merely the latest), "Leave me alone, I don't want to speak to you." And she had learned how to add, if necessary, "Go away or I'll call a policeman." Of course, when Patrick was with them, there was no problem. He was big and tall and looked as though he could knock anybody flat in two minutes. But she didn't always want to be with Patrick, going where he wanted to go, leaving when he was ready to leave, trying to keep up with his long-legged stride. She tried to explain to him (and although Maggie was not that way herself, she did back her up) that she was not looking for adventure when she went off on her own — not sexual adventure anyway. She just liked moving along at her own pace, liked not feeling guilty if she wanted to forget plans that were made the night before and just sit in a café and watch the crowds. Sometimes, when she went walking, she got lost; but that was part of the fun of it, having to ask directions, to make oneself understood, to figure out the map where the street names had been Latinized (just to make it more difficult), but not the street signs, so that the main street they were living near, BEIKOY, for example, was spelt on the map more or less the way it was pronounced, VEIKOU.

"*You* know," Johanna said to Patrick, defending her desire to spend some time exploring on her own, "it's the sort of thing that you like to do."

"But I'm a *man*," Patrick said quickly and they all three howled with laughter. He really didn't like her to go off—or so it seemed to Johanna—because then, who would stay with Maggie, if he wanted to take off on his own (as he often did)?

In the first week, they had tried for one day to all go their separate ways, move at their own pace and according to their own whims, agreeing to meet up at Zonar's restaurant in the late afternoon. But Maggie had been frightened by the men, one in particular who followed her all through the Plaka, and she said that, next time, she'd stay at the pension and read. She said that she knew that it was silly and cowardly, but it wasn't worth it—not for her. They could see that she had been crying. She was not one of those women who look particularly attractive when they cry and Johanna believed in Maggie's tears.

"And the crowds," Maggie said, "the crowds are terrible."

"'Agoraphobia,'" Johanna said, "fear of the marketplace. A good Greek word. Apparently lots more women suffer from it than men."

"Well, in this case, when they look at you as if you were part of the produce, I think that fear is justified!"

"It's okay, Muggins," Patrick said, looking at her fondly, "we won't desert you again."

At that moment, Johanna experienced an emotion which she first felt back in fourth grade when she had won a spelling bee and been mocked by the boys at recess. It had dawned on her, then, that it didn't pay for a girl to be too smart. Patrick never used that tone of voice with *her*, never gave *her* a Patrick-invented nickname (actually, no one had ever given Johanna a nickname), never looked at *her* protectively. But did she want that? she asked herself. And a small voice said, "Well, once in a while."

They had now been in Greece three weeks and Maggie still couldn't remember the word for "thank you." "Because one of us is always there," Johanna thought, "like a prompter, standing in the wings. And because Patrick likes it that way; it flatters him that she can't remember."

What Johanna couldn't decide was whether the not-remembering was somewhat deliberate on Maggie's part. Hadn't they both been brought up to flatter men? Wasn't that how you "got" a man, really, by making him feel important?

"You can catch more flies with honey than with vinegar." Johanna could still hear her mother's voice. "Don't be so proud, Johanna."

"I'll just finish this chapter," Patrick said to her from the other bed. "I couldn't read on the train."

"No," she said, "you were too busy practicing your Greek on the man with the brother in Montréal." She knew that what he really wanted was to make sure that Maggie was asleep in the other room before they began making love. It was Maggie's night to sleep alone. Johanna wondered for the hundredth time in the past month just why she was continuing with this absurdly futile proceeding. And for the hundredth time, she ignored the answer.

She smiled sweetly across at Patrick. "I don't mind if you read," she said. "I'm pretty sleepy after all that retsina at dinner. I just may fall asleep." That would make him squirm a little. What would *that* do to their precious schedule? Would she get a raincheck or would it be like losing your place in the queue? The man on the train had asked Patrick which of the two women was his wife?

Patrick grinned at her. "I know how to wake you up."

"Don't be so sure," she said, and suddenly angry, rolled over and turned towards the wall, pulling the covers up over her head. She could hear the workmen out in the corridor, laughing and throwing dice. They were just starting to play when Patrick and Maggie and Johanna came back from dinner in the village.

"*Tavli*," one of the men said, pointing to the board. It was backgammon.

"That's interesting," Johanna said. "Tables? That's the old English name as well. Chaucer talks about the Canterbury pilgrims playing at 'tables.' I wonder if the Wife of Bath played too; it seems to be such a man's game here."

The men invited them to sit down; they had a large aluminum pitcher of retsina on the floor and they were already a little bit drunk. Johanna was surprised when Patrick declined. "Tired," he said smiling, "sleep." He folded his hands beneath one cheek.

"*Kimithó*," Johanna said and Patrick gave her a dirty look. The men laughed heartily, looking at the two women.

"*Kalli-níchta*," they said grinning, "*kalli-níchta*. Goodnight."

"You don't want to improve your game?" Johanna said sweetly. Patrick chose to ignore this.

"We really had better turn in. The taxi's supposed to come at half-past eight and the landlord said that he'd give us breakfast at eight."

He and Johanna paused at one door; Maggie at the next. The workmen had not resumed their game, as they were watching the three foreigners with great interest. That's when Maggie asked Johanna to come down the hall with her to the lavatories.

"Sure," Johanna said, "I have to go anyway. Just a minute, while I get my stuff."

"It's silly," Maggie said to her in the washroom. "But I was really afraid to come down here alone. And I think that I've got the trots again," she added, trying to laugh.

Johanna imagined Maggie in her nightgown, knocking on their door, embarrassed, wondering if she were interrupting anything, if they were still awake. How indulgent would Patrick feel if he were awakened in the middle of the night?

"Look," she said, "if you're that scared, why don't we change places?" Johanna could see that Maggie's hands were actually trembling. God knows, she wouldn't want to knock on *their* door, if the situation were reversed as it had been in Delphi, when Johanna was the one on her own.

The bus trip up had been spectacular, but hair-raising, so after lunch, they agreed to take a rest before exploring. Patrick and Maggie offered to knock on Johanna's door at three o'clock, but they didn't come. They still hadn't come by three-thirty, so Johanna, convinced that they were screwing, forced herself to go out and not wait there imagining things. There was virtually no one in the town and she found herself enjoying the walk. Patrick finally caught up with her. She was sitting on a rock, looking down hundreds of feet, into the ravine below.

"We went to get you and couldn't find you," he said smiling. ("You smug bastard," she thought to herself.)

"That's all right. I've been for a long walk. It really is like the centre of the world."

He sat down and put his arm around her. "I want you to know that I love you."

"Whatever *that* means," she said. "From one of these rocks, they used to throw down people who were guilty of sacrilege. Aren't we lucky that we live in a more advanced age?"

"The reason that we were late," he began, but she interrupted him.

"For God's sake, Patrick, you don't have to give me the *reason*. This whole thing is getting too much like a railway schedule."

"The reason that we were late was because Maggie was crying."

"So what else is new?" she said.

"That's not at all nice."

"I'm not 'nice,' Patrick. I thought that we'd already established that fact. And I *am* sorry for that remark, but I was in a pretty good mood sitting here, thinking about those old Greeks, and now, I'm in a pretty bad mood thinking about you and me and Maggie. I know perfectly well why she's crying; I cry too."

"She really likes you, you know."

"Yes, I know, thank you — and I like her too. In any other circumstances, we would probably be the best of friends."

"If I weren't in the way."

"Exactly. If you weren't in the way."


"Oh, we can't switch now," Maggie said, "it would make things too complicated."

"No, it wouldn't. We'd just switch days. It's easy, really."

She hesitated. "Patrick would be angry."

"No, he wouldn't. He'd be only too happy to protect you."

She hadn't meant that last remark to come out so sarcastically.

"What do you mean?"

"Oh, nothing. Forget it! Let's just go back and switch over. We don't need to move our packs or anything."

"No," Maggie said slowly. "They're just workmen who are having a good time. I'm dumb to be afraid."

"In this instance, I suspect that you are. What could happen with us right here?"

"You're right, nothing. Nothing at all!"

"One little yell and we'd come running."

(If Patrick were there, he would have pointed out that *that* wasn't a particularly 'nice' thing to say either.)

"I'm going to put a chair under my door handle," Maggie said, trying to laugh at herself again.

"All right. And just knock on the wall if you have to go in the night. I promise that I'll get up and come with you."

"Thanks." (Although they both knew that Maggie would never do it.)

She could hear, even if she couldn't understand, every word that was coming from the players in the corridor. The walls were thin. This was the first time that they'd taken adjacent rooms. They were lucky at the pension in Athens. They had been given rooms downstairs, in the oldest part of the house, facing each other across a broad terrazzo hall. There were heavy doors and the rooms were virtually soundproof, except for the noise coming in from the street. Athenians were night people and the street was not really quiet until almost dawn. They didn't mind; it made any other stray sounds just part of the general racket. For official purposes, Johanna and Maggie were in one room and Patrick was in the other. Nobody paid much attention to them, except for a handsome Australian woman who had rented a room for the entire winter and who eyed them thoughtfully over the breakfast table. Johanna wondered if the landlady, an English woman who married an Istanbul Greek, had noticed that there were come stains on all the sheets and mentioned it to the Australian woman. They seemed to be good friends. It made them a bit uneasy to be looked at in that cool, speculative way. The pension was full for Christmas and they promised to be back for a big party on Christmas Eve. Even before they left, great boars, their coats still on, hung down outside the butchers on Athenas Street, and a neon dove wished everyone *Hrónia Polla,* "many years," in Syntagma Square. Christmas was not a big event for the Greeks, their landlady told them; New Year's was much more important. But Christmas Eve was the one day of the year that she herself felt really homesick and Dmitri enjoyed an English party; he liked all things English.

"We will get big turkey," he said. "With all insides still in, head, feets still on. You women will sit in kitchen like pee-sants; we mans will get drunk."

"I must make some New Year's resolutions," Johanna thought, nearly asleep. "One in particular—one big one!"

On the day before they left Athens, it was snowing a little. They had been walking down Veikou, arm in arm, Patrick in the middle, of course, wrapped up in their new Greek sweaters (It had never occurred to them that Athens would be cold; "You would think that one of us would have paid attention in Social Studies," Patrick said), very excited, talking about the coming trip. They had just been shopping—Johanna and Maggie, for Patrick; Patrick and Maggie, for Johanna; Johanna and Patrick, for Maggie, while she sat in a *taverna* that they liked, near the Tower of the Winds.

As they were walking along, suddenly Maggie stuck her arm out and bent it at the wrist.

"What are you doing?" Patrick asked. She did look strange with her arm sticking out like that.

"Practicing," she said.

"?"

"Well, it needn't stop with you always in the middle, needn't it? I might find another fellow that I wanted to bring in; Johanna might. There could be a whole string of us—like a chorus line."

Johanna, delighted, stuck her left arm out and draped it over an imaginary shoulder. People were turning around to look.

"Ha ha," Patrick said, "very funny." But they could see that he was a little bit shaken. The idea had never occurred to him.

"Maggie's right," Johanna said. "Why stop with a ménage à trois? Why not a ménage à cinq? Three men and two women."

"A sept," Maggie suggested.

"Neuf!"

"Onze!"

They began to giggle. Johanna thought that she had never liked Maggie better than at this moment. Poor old Patrick. What would really finish him would be if she and Maggie got it on and went off and left him!

"Fucking bitches!" Patrick said, but he, too, was laughing.

When she was nearly asleep, Patrick crawled into bed with her. His feet were cold. She had been lying in a strange half-dream, the imagery of which, obviously influenced by the daunting rocks which rose above them just beyond the village and the weird valley that they were now in. The landscape of her dream was full of great masses of naked rock and the voices of the men in the corridor had become the voices of black-robed men who were somehow deciding her fate. She was wearing a brilliant orange dress and somehow that was not "allowed." Although she could not understand the voices of the men, monks probably, called into being by her careful reading of the *Blue Guide* that afternoon, she knew that the orange dress was not "allowed." It was like something out of Bosch, her dream, and she was grateful for Patrick's bulk, cold feet and all.

"You've got awfully cold feet," she whispered, turning towards him. She had felt his erection against her back.

"Come warm me up."

"Oh yes," she said, grateful to be rescued, "I'll warm you up all right."

They were just getting going when Johanna heard a sound from next door. A sob. There was no mistaking what it was—or who it was.

"Patrick," she whispered against his ear, "Maggie's crying."

They lay still. There it was again. Johanna sighed.

"Look, I think that you'd better go and spend the rest of the night with her. Maybe she's got the trots and she's afraid to go down the hall."

She couldn't see Patrick's face in the darkness and she had no idea what he was thinking.

"Do you think so?"

"I do."

He gave her breast a squeeze and got out of bed.

"You're not so bad after all," he said. She could hear him fumbling around for his clothes.

"Put the light on," she said. "I'm wide awake now." And as

he moved to the door, she said, "And I'm not 'nice,' just practical. It wouldn't have been any good."

"See you in the morning," he whispered. "God knows what those guys in the hall are going to think."

"They'll probably report us to the monks." She reached up and turned off the light.

And then, when he was gone, she turned the light back on again. "This really can't go on," she thought, "it really can't." She got up, naked, and went over and made Patrick's bed. Then, she straightened out her own and turned off the light once more. She pulled back the heavy curtains and could see, by the moon, all the rough beginnings of the addition that the workmen were building, and then, beyond, the dark masses of the cliffs and rocks of Meteora. Tomorrow, they would go up and look at the monasteries that still remained open. Johanna didn't like heights and was not really looking forward to it. Apparently, they had to climb up steep steps that were cut in the rock. Maybe she would light a beeswax candle and ask forgiveness for what she was about to do. She heard somebody bump against the wall next door. What if she, now, were to give a little sob? What would they do? What if she shouted, "I can hear you in there, you fuckers!" Just at the appropriate moment. She felt absolutely full of rage, like a balloon that has been blown up and blown up and blown up until —. Until. She began to dress in the dark.

The men were surprised to see her. An empty pitcher stood beside a full one, but they didn't seem any more drunk than they were two hours ago.

She smiled at them. "I want to play," she said. She had looked up how to say it.

They stared at her, not quite smiling. "That mans," said the biggest of the men, "that mans is your husbands?"

"No," she said, "*óshi*. He is my *athelphos*—my brother."

They began to laugh then, and one of them shook his head at her. "No, no. Brother no like. You go sleeps."

She held out her hand for the dice. "It's okay," she said, "*endaksi*. My brother says that it's okay."

The men looked at one another and then shrugged. They offered her a packing case on which to sit. She knew that she had ruined their game, but that was not the point. She wanted Patrick to hear her out in the corridor, wanted him to be aware of her, not so much to put him off *his* game, as to get it over with—all this—to begin the last and fatal throw.

And, oh God, she was horny enough! If one of them really should go against all his instincts, all that he'd been taught, and really think her "brother" had said that it was okay, then she wasn't going to say no. And she wasn't going to keep her voice down either. She was tired of keeping her voice down.

She imagined the workman's strong hands running over her body, imagined him pausing at her belly. "*Omphalos*," he would say, circling her bellybutton with the hard tips of his fingers, "*omphalos*," the centre. And the two of them laughing, as he pushed her legs apart, he saying the words in Greek, she repeating them. "You like this?" "Yes." "It please you?" "Yes." "*Temenos*," she would say, "the sacred enclosure." "*Iereos*," she would say. "The priest." "The priest enters the sacred enclosure."

Patrick and Maggie, on the other side of the wall, wouldn't be able to make out the words. They would hear only the laughter and the murmur of two voices. She held out her hand for the dice. "*Endaksi*," the bigger man said. They threw to see who would start.


The next morning, Johanna was up and pouring honey onto her bread when Maggie and Patrick appeared from the other room. They ate at the small table in the corridor, fresh eggs and bread and honey. The workmen were already hammering away outside.

When the landlord brought their coffee, he looked at Johanna and Maggie in their blue jeans and shook his head. He said something in Greek to Patrick.

"*Thín sás kataláveno*," Patrick said. "I don't understand you."

The landlord pointed to the women in their jeans and pointed up towards Meteora. He said something that sounded like "*foot-sa*," then pointed at the jeans again.

"Oh, I know," Johanna said, "skirt! We have to wear skirts."

She mimed putting on a skirt and the man nodded. "We'd better hurry and change."

"I don't have a skirt with me," Maggie said sadly.

"Maybe we could borrow one from the landlord's wife?"

Patrick was in a terrible mood. "Just do something," he said, "the taxi will be here any minute." He glared at Johanna. "Didn't it say anything in the *Blue Guide*?"

"Nothing about wearing skirts or I would've mentioned it."

It turned out the landlord's wife was away. Maggie offered to stay behind, but they said nonsense. Then Johanna offered to stay behind and let Maggie have her skirt. It was a wrap-around and would fit anybody. She said that she didn't like heights anyway. Patrick gave Johanna a really terrible look and Maggie looked uncomfortable.

"I don't think you should stay behind, Johanna. Not after we've come all this way."

"I could go after you two come back. We could make some sort of deal with the taxi-driver."

"We're all going together," Patrick said, "or none of us is going."

Then Maggie had a brainwave. She told Patrick to go and get his long raincape. She was so small, it would cover her completely. She rolled her jeans up and put on long socks.

"I look eccentric," she said, "but I imagine the monks are used to that."

"You certainly can't tell that you've got trousers on," Johanna said. "Just be careful when you sit down. And if there's lots of steps, one of us should climb in front of you and one behind. Just in case."

The taxi honked. In order to get down to the road, they had to pass the workmen, who greeted them very formally.

"Good morning," Johanna said in Greek.

Patrick and Maggie said nothing. Maggie got into the taxi first and arranged the cape around her, then Patrick got in the front seat and Johanna got in next to Maggie. It was very cold and the mist hung low over the great masses of naked rock above them. Johanna shivered.

"*Endaksi*," Patrick said, "let's go."

Johanna leaned out the window and waved at the workmen.
"You fucking bitch!" Patrick said. "You fucking bitch!"

"It's all right, Patrick," Johanna said, "I told them that you were my brother."

Then she opened the *Blue Guide* and began to read out loud to her companions.

# OUT IN THE MIDDAY SUN

The Majestic was one of the old pre-Independence hotels dating back to the early days of the Kenya-Uganda Railway, and it had, among other delights (such as the option not to have noisy air conditioning, if one did not wish it, to have the far more picturesque and soothing—if less efficient—three-bladed fans that they had read about so often in Maugham and Graham Greene), a wide vine-shaded verandah that extended on all four sides. And so she didn't see him at first, for she had come out onto the front verandah, whereas her husband was seated at the back, which overlooked the lush garden, head bent over a blue aerogramme, writing swiftly and easily, oblivious to everything except his thoughts, which seemed to her, watching him, to transfer themselves, automatically, from his mind onto the paper. It was as if the black pen (the pen that he used for more than twenty years) were magic, like the broom of "the sorcerer's apprentice."

The small glass table upon which he was writing held a tea tray (pushed to one side), a pile of books (on top, his ubiquitous black notebook), a camera and the ridiculous bush hat, with its fake leopard skin band, which he bought for a joke in Nairobi. All of the other tables, all of the other comfortable wicker chairs with their faded chintz cushions, were deserted—

except for one. In exactly the opposite corner to her husband, as though by some mutual agreement, sat a red-faced man in shorts and an open shirt, reading a paper and sucking on an unlit pipe.

"He is another South African," she thought, "and when I ask him if he is finished with his paper, he will say, 'Yis,' in that horrible South African accent, and then maybe, he will tell us stories of how the country's gone to pot since the blacks took over." There had been one South African sharing their table on the train last night, an ex-Kenyan, who had left ten years before. When Frank asked him if the Masai had changed much over the years, he said, "They still stink, if that's what you mean." He told them that Americans and Canadians did a lot of harm, for they wanted to treat the black man as an equal and he wasn't, he simply wasn't. "A good chap," the man said, buttering a cracker, "so long as he's led." She had been very conscious, all of a sudden, of the smooth brown hand of the dining-car steward, deftly pouring her coffee as the train swayed from side to side. Surely, he had overheard? Surely, the two dark businessmen at the next table had also heard? The fear that had subsided for a bit, with the excitement of the train journey, came back to her at that moment, as though she had swallowed a stone, as though someone behind her had silently laid a heavy hand on her bare shoulder. She told Frank that she was going to find her cardigan, and got up hurriedly, almost running by the time she reached the end of the car. He stayed, talking to the man for hours — it was all "material" to go in the black notebook — while she lay on her narrow bunk, pretending to read by the dull lamp, but knowing that something terrible was going to happen, that whatever laid its heavy hand on her bare arm could follow her through locked doors.

("How would you like to wind up this year by going to see some elephants?" he said to her in Athens. And she, who had been screwing up her courage to tell him about the letter, who had come into his study with coffee and cakes and the letter in her pocket, took a deep breath and smiled, and said, "Elephants, why not?" The next day, they had gone to the British Council Library — or she had gone there — and she got out Karen Blixen's *Out of Africa*; then she went to the American bookshop for

Hemingway. For she knew that, as soon as she told him, he would leave her. And a selfish part of her said, "Why not see Africa first?")

The air on the verandah smelled fresh and cool. It had rained while she was asleep; it rained every day now, but only for a little while. It rained with such fierceness that raincoats or umbrellas were really quite useless. Mould grew inside of shoes, the wives at the High Commission told her, and one's feet were never really clean. But she didn't mind; she wouldn't be out here long enough to mind. It got hotter and hotter, until the sun which, in Canada, she never considered as anything other than a friendly force, burned with a fierceness that made her feel as if the whole world were suddenly going to burst into flame. Any minute now, she would look down and find the hem of her dress on fire —or her shoes, or even her hair. And, at that instant, when she could almost see the landscape begin to flicker and burn, the heavy rains began.

"It's almost sexual," Frank said—and it was.

(As soon as she told him, he would leave her. Oh, not physically, of course, that would come later, but he would leave her just the same; he would begin the inevitable withdrawal. She would show him the letter, deeply creased and rather dirty from folding and unfolding, and he would read it, frowning slightly in that shortsighted way he had, and then, he would read it again and reach across the table to put his big hand over her small one, or get up, very formally, very picturesquely, and come round to her chair and kiss her and call for champagne and tell the whole world—whether or not the whole world was interested—and then, he would realize the significance of the date and the questions would begin, whimsical at first: "I guess I should say, 'How long has this been going on'?" but getting more and more serious and probing, as he got more and more drunk. And his big hands would clench and unclench until he put them under the table, so that the others wouldn't see. And then, it would be all over. She was glad it wasn't a real shooting safari that they were going on. She had read her Hemingway. Suppose he blew the back of her head off?)

Now, the earth still steamed from the rains, and the air was cool and heavy with the smell of flowers and something else—a sweet overripe smell, slightly rotten, like the smell of childhood Augusts and windfall apples lying rotting in the grass—only less pleasant. Two young girls, wrapped in pieces of brightly printed cloth, were standing under a jacaranda tree in the garden, bending stiff-legged over a basket of linen, their round little bottoms clearly visible under the tight fabric, raising up, bending, folding. The earth steamed around them and the sun poured down through the blue flowers, splashing light along their bare arms. They chattered and giggled as they worked. What did they giggle about? she wondered. Boys, most probably. ("Now, I'll be able to have girlfriends again," she thought, "friends of my own.")

She crossed swiftly to where her husband was still writing, using a second aerogramme now. Was he writing to one of them, one of his admiring female students? Describing this morning's incident? To which one was he writing with such concentration that he was missing the scene under the tree? (But those African girls wouldn't be impressed with him, would they? Or not for the right reasons—his reasons.) She kissed the top of his head and noticed, for the first time, how thin his hair was. Maybe the bush hat wasn't such a joke after all; maybe the sun really hurt his head and he didn't want to admit it. She suddenly felt a great rush of affection for him.

He started guiltily, looked around at her and quickly turned the letter over. Her affection disappeared.

"Which one is it?" she said sweetly. "The one with the big tits who writes sonnets or the one with the Botticelli hair who chooses to write in more open forms?"

She sat down in the chair opposite him and offered him a brilliant smile. He, in his turn, ignored her question. She didn't like herself at this moment. She didn't like her voice or her silly smile. She was like some clever brittle woman in a Noel Coward play.

"Listen, did you know that when Teddy Roosevelt set out on his post-presidential safari, he took along a hundred porters all dressed in blue shirts? Why blue shirts? I thought that safari people were always supposed to wander through the jungle in elephant-grey or dried-earth brown or giant-fern green. And not even red, white and blue—just blue. Sounds apocryphal, don't you think? The man wasn't a fool. After all, he'd been President and he'd also shot all kinds of things, all over the place. He was one of those real hunters, like Hemingway, one of those who didn't mind killing, so long as they killed cleanly—or something like that."

And, all the time that he was saying this, making her smile in spite of herself, staring into her eyes, like a magician who wants to divert your attention, his hands were busy folding the aerogramme into thirds, then again and again, until it was not much bigger than a packet of cigarette papers. And, this done, thrusting it into his shirt pocket.

"Why don't you finish your letters?" she said. "I didn't mean to interrupt."

"I'd rather look at you. Are you feeling better? You look as if you were feeling better."

"Much much better. You have no idea how much better. I feel like a new woman."

"I liked the old one."

"Did you?" She gave him another smile, tossed it to him, a small gift. She felt as if she had stepped back a great distance and was really looking at him for the first time in five years. "He is getting old," she thought, "or old-er. He is getting older and he is afraid. Because of my own fear, I didn't see it. Any day now, he will suggest that I have a baby." And then, she thought (she almost said right out loud), "Write her a good one. Don't let her get away." Instead, she said, "Why don't I write a letter, too? My mother's going to think that I've been swallowed by a lion. Do you have any gorilla prints left?"

He leafed through a pile of unused aerogrammes.

"Nope. We can get some tomorrow though. I've got two rhinoceroses, one Thomson's gazelle and a young wart hog, but I'm saving that for our beloved chairman. Why not write a regular letter? I went to the post office and bought some beautiful stamps. Or, let's not write letters at all; I'm tired of writing letters."

"Is it too early to have a drink?"

"That's like the difference between 'can I' and 'may I.' It's never too early to have a drink; the question is whether or not the bar is open."

She was surprised. Ordinarily, he would know exactly when the bar was open. The letter must have been important. He beckoned to a white-jacketed steward, who was clearing away discarded tea things and plumping up the cushions. (The red-faced man had disappeared.)

"What'll you have, Mama?" They had been calling each other Mama and Papa as a joke.

"Just a beer."

"That's good. Listen to this. Mzuri," he said. "Nataka tembo baridi. Tembo mbili. Tusker. Mbili tusker."

The boy grinned at him and went away.

"He's probably gone to get an interpreter," she said.

"Ha ha. But really, weren't you impressed?"

"Terribly impressed. Awfully impressed."

"I've been practicing while you were asleep. Funny, how the word for beer and the word for elephant are the same. I wonder why? But it's a simple language, really. Verbs. Tenses. Very simple and economical. The nouns work with prefixes and there are a few different classes. Singular class one take M prefix; plurals Wa. Adjectives agree with nouns. Wife, Mke. Wives, Wake. Good wife, Mke mzuri. Good wives, Wake wazuri. I'll spare you further examples for the present."

His magician's patter went on and on. A long way away, in the town, she could hear the chanting of a muezzin—long, drawn out, compelling. There is but one God. And only one prophet at a time. She had been intending to wait until they got back home; after this morning, that was no longer possible. The muezzin's wail reminded her of this. "And yet, I am the infidel," she thought. "How strange."

"It will be dark soon," she said. "Shall we take the ferry over to one of those beach hotels for dinner? Eat with all the Germans?"

People told them about the Germans. How they came to the coast on package tours, and then ate and ate and ate, until there was no real profit. "They are in Greece, too," Frank said. "If the

94

Greeks see that you are European, they address you first in German. It's not just the war, but the almighty Deutsche Mark. It's amazing."

"Walk along the beach in the moonlight?" she asked. "Kiss beneath the Southern Cross?"

(This morning, after he got up and put his trousers on, kissed her closed eyes and tiptoed away, she lay there in the darkened room, her thighs still wet with him, and she faced her fear. She faced it and it slunk away. Her fear had nothing to do with Africa. That was what she had known all along. Africa, like a dream, had simply provided the symbols. She had refused to recognize the reality behind them. She had to leave him. She loved him, but she had to leave; it was as simple as that. The fear had begun before they ever stepped on the plane; before he ever mentioned elephants or Africa. The fear had begun with a parcel sent out under a false name. The heavy hand on her shoulder was her own.)

The steward brought them their drinks.

"'This, the first one of the day, the finest one there is'."

"*Green Hills of Africa*," she said. "Do you suppose Hemingway really talked like that?"

"Asante sana," he said to the steward, "and in ten minutes, two others."

"What happened to your Swahili?"

"Mzuri," he said, "two others. Two more, mzuri."

"Sure, he talked like that. He came back with his porters and pals and took a bath in the portable bath and washed all the blood off his hands and put on his mosquito boots and called for beer and Mama and they sat there, drinking beer and listening to the hyenas screaming, and talked like that."

"God. What do you suppose mosquito boots looked like?"

"Mosquito colour. Made out of crushed female anopheles. Your feet glowed in the dark."

"That's fireflies, you idiot." And then, "Hemingway had a lot of wives, didn't he? Do you think that he talked about the same thing with all his wives? Do you think that any of them ever met — at the Ritz Bar or wherever — and got together and compared what he was like in bed, or laughed at him behind his back?"

(Frank had two other wives before her. There had always been the tacit understanding that the line did not necessarily stop there. "He's really fun," she thought now, "and attractive. He draws you in. Especially if you are young and uncertain and eager for kisses and praise. But he is the kind of man who will love you only so long as you walk a few steps behind. Only so long as you arrange the dinners and the airline tickets, and the Christmas presents to all the far-flung children.")

She had been his most brilliant student. It came over her, almost like nausea, the sudden suspicion that perhaps he had married her to shut her up. "When he marries big tits or the other one," she thought, "everyone will say that it's because they are young and beautiful and he is growing old." But that's not it — or not the whole of it. "They are brilliant. I am brilliant. For five years, I have been pretending to be that which I am not." He thought while he laboured away in a rented flat in Athens that she was going, every morning, to the Lyceum of Greek Women, where she was learning ethnic dances. And all the time she was sitting in a tiny storage room, windowless, almost airless, next to the British Council Reading Room, head down over a table bought at a flea market, concentrating, writing. He never asked her to dance for him; she counted on the fact that he wouldn't.

"Where are you?" he said.

She hesitated, flustered. "In Athens."

"I hope that you weren't bored there. I know that it must have been lonely for you at times."

"Not really. I love Greece. There were winter afternoons when I was the only person on the Acropolis, except for the guard. I expected Poseidon or Athena to come around the corner at any minute. I wasn't bored."

The chant of the muezzin went on and on and on.

("I'm afraid," she whispered against his shoulder, their first night in Nairobi. "Afraid of what?" he said in his high, rather nasal voice. "Afraid of snakes — of scorpions, of spiders?"

"I don't know, I don't know, I don't know."

"It's not like you to be afraid," he said. And then, inevitably, "Come here, I know how to make you relax.")

96

But it wasn't just her fear of leaving him. There was something in the eyes of the people. There were stories—everybody had one. A woman had been driving alone along the Nairobi-Mombasa road. A gang of thieves, wielding pangas, forced her off the road and demanded money. And her gold necklace. And her watch. She handed them all over.

But she wouldn't give them her wedding ring. She refused to give that up. She knew some Swahili, for she had lived in the district a long time, all her married life. She tried to explain to them about the wedding ring. Nevertheless, they cut her finger off and left her there, in the noon haze, screaming.

Everyone seemed to know this woman or know someone who knew her. In the bar of the New Stanley Hotel, in the Norfolk Hotel bar, at dinner parties arranged by the High Commission, she listened politely to what was being said, while her eyes constantly sought out women's hands—hands holding drinks or adjusting necklaces, hands patting the sleeve of a husband. She was always on the look-out for the nine-fingered woman who, everyone had assured her, had stayed. She wanted to ask her something—a couple of things. She wanted to talk to her.

("It's come!" said the girl behind the counter at American Express in Athens. "Your letter." Her dark eyes were dancing; to her, the pseudonym implied a lover. She took the letter in its crisp, white, expensive envelope and walked carefully down the stairs and out to one of the open-air cafés on the square. For an hour, she sat there, amid the tourists and coffee cups, the unopened letter in her lap.

"How long has this been going on?" he would say, laughing. "Darling, I think that it's wonderful.")

They spent the morning at Fort Jesus, and then they wandered through the Old Town, past shops of moneylenders, tinsmiths, goldsmiths; past black-robed women who pressed themselves against the walls, or retreated into dim alleys, as the foreigners passed.

"I feel like I'm in Casablanca," Frank said. "Not East Africa."

"Or Elizabethan England. Look at those balconies." But she didn't really like it. It was too hot, too narrow, too smelly.

"Look at that sign," he said. "'Super Quality Non-Alcoholic

Natural Flowers 300 Verities Perfumes.' I didn't know there were that many verities." He held his notebook against a peeling yellow wall and wrote in it while she glanced nervously around.

"What is wrong with me?" she thought. "What is the matter with me?"

It was like a labyrinth. The heat was intense; her "English breakfast," included in their bill, sat heavily on her stomach. She wanted to go back, but she was too ashamed to say so. Her wedding ring seemed to glitter invitingly and she felt that dark eyes, hostile eyes, watched her from every alley and recessed doorway.

They shouldn't be here. They came to a mosque and Frank wanted to go in.

"I can't," she said miserably, "You know that. I'll have to wait out here. Maybe you could come back?"

He looked at her bare arms. "I guess you can't at that. I'll only be a minute. You don't really mind?"

"Of course, I mind, but go ahead." This last to his disappearing back.

She had to find some shade, a place to sit down — or she would begin to scream. Three children in faded rags appeared and asked her for shillingi. They giggled and ran away.

There was nothing else but silence, and a faint humming that might have been insects, that might have been inside her head. "I'm going mad," she thought. "So this is what it's like."

Then the leper appeared, out of nowhere, or so it seemed, pulling himself along with a kind of scything motion, one mutilated leg stuck straight ahead, a bizarre tiller, the good leg and one good arm, on the opposite side, doing all the work. He moved remarkably fast and she stood on the steps of the mosque, horrified, knowing that this was, after all, what she had been waiting for.

One eye hung out of its socket. She did not think of running; she could not. He swung himself up the broad steps and stopped just below where she was standing. He touched her bare foot with what was left of a hand and she gasped. It was like a polished mahogany walking stick, that arm and hand. Even as she felt the nausea rise, she could not shut her eyes. He began to beg, whining at her in Arabic, and holding out his good hand, the dreadful eye lolling against his brown cheek.

"Go away," she said desperately, fumbling with her purse. "Please. Go away."

He rubbed her bare leg and she vomited all over the step, just as Frank came running down.

"Get him away from me!"

"It's all right. He's not dangerous. It's all right."

He led her, sobbing, back down the narrow streets, while a small boy, promised a suitable reward, ran for a taxi.

Back at the hotel, she turned on him. "Are you going to write about that, too? About your wife vomiting in the street in Mombasa?"

"Don't be silly," he said. But she could see from his eyes that it would go down in the black notebook with the three hundred verities and the South African man and the name of the local beer.

(Feeling the sickness rise in her throat, mortified, humiliated, she managed to turn her head, so that she would at least spare the poor creature below her. And, in that instant, she saw the feet of her husband, the feet and the bottoms of his trousers, and knew that he had been standing there, watching her, watching the scene, the broken hand against her white dress; enjoying the composition. He only came forward to help when it was too late.)

She stood up. "I'm going to put on some sensible shoes," she said, "if we're actually going walking on the beach."

"I'll order a taxi for 5:30," he said, "and then, I'll come and tidy up."

She knew that he wanted to finish his letter.

Up in the room, brushing her hair in front of the mirror-fronted wardrobe, she stared at her solemn reflection. She could still change her mind. Did he not offer her something more valuable than this strange freedom that she was opting for? This morning, she hated him; now, she forgave him completely. Didn't she have to forgive him completely? Wasn't that the point? For she was opting to be just like him, wasn't she?

"Aren't you?" she said to the woman in the mirror.

He offered her his talent and his need, and in return, she was

99

to be there, real flesh, real blood, to respond to both. He used everything as subject; why should she be excepted?

But she had betrayed him. She had lived in his house and slept in his bed, and yet, for the past few years, she had kept the essential part of herself hidden from him, out of his reach. She had been like that woman, there, in the mirror—a splendid imitation of herself.

She would tell him when they got to the game reserve tomorrow. She would tell him at sundown, beneath the eternal snows of Kilimanjaro. He couldn't fail to appreciate the appropriateness.

He would call for champagne, as the last rays of the sun hit the fabulous mountain. And she would not look at his stricken face.

Or would she? Would she notice every little detail of his pain, the way his hands clenched and unclenched (perhaps he would even break the stem of his glass), the whole terrible bravado of his celebration.

Would she notice all that, and then, when she got free of him, write about that, too?

# TIMBUKTU

"...up the river to Timbuktu." For the past few minutes, she had been doing a jellyfish float, head down and arms around her knees, bobbing just below the surface of the water, like a cork. The sea was a little too warm, a little too sticky, to be really pleasant, but it was better than going back and sitting under the striped umbrella with Mrs. Avis, and hearing, once again, about Sabina's malocclusion or the latest piece of villainy on the part of the Avis' cook-steward. She had just stood up and was shaking the water out of her ears when she heard—or thought that she heard—the end of somebody's sentence: "...up the river to Timbuktu." "Rivah," the voice said, "up the rivah." She looked around. The glare from the water was almost unbearable and she had to squint. Several people were near enough to have been overheard: a solitary overly-tanned woman who was lying face down on a blue and orange Lilo; she was the closest, but there was no one for her to speak *to*, so the brown, ringed hand of the woman paddled with tiny movements, directing the air mattress away from the shore. Anyway, she thought that it had been a man's voice; soft and southern, yes, but definitely male. Where was he? Who was going up the rivah to Timbuktu? Perhaps because her ears were full of water, perhaps because she had been disgruntled when they set out for the beach, the words presented themselves to her with a strange, almost symbolic force. "Timbuktu-ou-ou." Curiously erotic and beckoning, like the sound of doves and train whistles calling through the open bedroom windows of her childhood.

A large beach ball landed with a thud and a splash in the water, just in front of her. She tossed it away, absentmindedly, not bothering to look around for the owner. The blue-green water was full of men and women and children, almost all of them white, and more couples and family groups were spread out on mats under the huge Air Afrique umbrellas. The men were enjoying a morning without work, for this was Sunday, and the women were worrying about what to have for Sunday lunch. "You will have a cook-steward," Philip said, a few days after he proposed to her, "and he'll do most of the cooking. Actually, I've had the same man for years. But it's always cold chop on Sundays — that's the usual day off." How strange, she thought, then, having a man for a servant, a man to clean and cook and put away the laundry (a washerman to do it). "Lucky you," Philip's mother said to her, just before they sailed. "Fancy having someone to do all your work for you." Philip's mother firmly believed that a woman's place was in the home. She was getting on, and yet, servantless, she still kept her house immaculate, tended a garden which was not only beautifully neat, but also well-known for its beauty of colour and texture and shape. She put up her own jams and jellies, did her washing on Monday, ironing Tuesday, mending Wednesday, baking Thursday, and walked three miles to the village every day to do her shopping. Three afternoons a week she played duplicate bridge. Philip's father was a retired grammar school teacher. He raised fuschias and long delicious English cucumbers in a greenhouse at the bottom of the garden. Every leave, Rona and Philip went back to Sussex to visit them. Rona wanted to go to some place like Abidjan or Accra, or maybe even drive to East Africa, but Philip pointed out, quite reasonably, that his parents were getting on and that he was their only son. And they did get up to London for several weekends. Philip bought new shorts and shirts, while Rona went to the Royal Academy show or the Victoria and Albert (her favourite museum), where she laughed over all the Victorian

102

sentimental paintings—a young soldier approaching a little group, around a simple gravestone, and the caption underneath which read: "Too Late." In the evenings, they went to plays. They both loved London, although it had become "wickedly expensive." It amused her to think to herself in the idiom of the English—"chop," "up to town," "super," "Sunday joint," "wickedly expensive." She couldn't say these things aloud without feeling self-conscious—even after all these years—but it amused her to think them. Out here, under the relentless clarity of the African sun, the English seemed so terribly, terribly English. Never mind, she probably seemed terribly, terribly Canadian—or American, she should say. To the British and Europeans, there was no real distinction. And yet, if she had said to a Scotsman, mistaking him for Welsh, "Oh well, it's all the same thing, isn't it?" he'd walk away in a fury and only refrain from knocking her down because she was a woman. And the children at the school where she taught, with their "Ta-ra, Miss" and cups of "tay" and "Our Mum, she," "Our Eddie, he," constantly saying to her, "Please, Miss, speak English," when she forgot and said truck for lorry or running shoes for plimsoles. Mrs. Avis, the wife of Philip's boss, had been in Dakar ten years and she still didn't speak more than a few words of French. Menu French and steward French, that's all. She prided herself on this fact and she wasn't the only wife like that. The husbands, of course, spoke the language—it was part of their job. But with the women, or some of them, it was as though, if they should learn to speak French, French *thoughts* might creep in. The fortress of smugness and insularity behind which they hid might be invaded or even overrun. Rona was terrified of becoming like these women; she practiced her own halting French every chance she got. And made such chances. Went, not just to Printania to do her shopping (where leeks hung in bunches, where perfect apples were mounted in pyramids so immaculate that one hesitated to disturb them, where one found imported pâté, imported wines, bins of bikinis, air conditioning, wives of French diplomats in chic little dresses, black bureaucrats in big sunglasses), but also to the market in Medina. There, she heard ordinary Africans speak French, as well as their own dialects, the French

103

an altogether different sounding thing from the Parisian French on the Plateau, the section of the city where the Europeans lived. The market sprawled out in front of her, crowded, noisy, smelly, hot. It both repelled and attracted. Small children ran after her saying, "Hey! Madame! Un p'tit cadeau!" Fat market women called out to her to buy their manioc or tomatoes or ground nuts. She would buy an orange, and 'whisk,' it was peeled, and a little plug cut out, so that she could suck at the sweet juice until all that was left was a soft pulpy sac. The market women laughed at her French and she knew that she was overcharged; but she persevered, and now, most of the regulars knew her—enquired after her health and showed her their "pickins," as Mrs. Avis and her friends would have called the fat, solemn little babies who slept in the shade of their mothers' stalls, or were bounced and fondled by an older brother or sister. Philip wanted a child. It was hard to use the word "desperately" about someone as calm and self-contained as Philip, but it was the word that occurred to her. He was more than twenty years older than she was—it wasn't just his parents who were "getting on." Each time that they went on leave, his mother made some oblique reference to the childlessness of Rona and Philip, and she always felt a little sorry for Philip as he maintained that this was a joint decision.

"We need time to get to know one another."

"Five years?" His mother smiled at them over her tapestry.

And when she saw the black babies, asleep on their mothers' backs, snug, secure, untroubled; or wide-eyed, gold earrings in their ears, hair done by an older sister or "Auntie" into a dozen intricate braids, it wasn't just her heart that lurched. It seemed to her that her very womb ached with longing. The fat market women laughed.

"Madame, combien d'enfants avez-vous? 'Ow many bébés?"

"Je n'en ai pas."

They would pat her flat stomach with their broad capable palms and some would offer her beads or little fetishes, recognizing the longing in her face and convinced that she was barren.

Why couldn't she then? What was holding her back? Just this morning, it had come up again. Jennifer Phelps was back from

England and they were supposed to go round for tea at four o'clock and see the baby. John had been interviewing nurse girls, although he knew that Jennifer would want to make the final choice herself. Philip got up early and made tea, as he always did on Sundays. He brought in the tray and sat down beside her on the bed. It was very early and the flat was still cold.

"You'd better get back in bed," she said, sitting up. "It's chilly." He smiled at her and stayed where he was. Philip's best features were his eyes, which were of an incredible clear blue — almost the blue of the clear unfaded sky of Dakar. He had put a bunch of violets (God knows what they must have cost him!) on the teatray. She reached out her hand to him.

"What lovely flowers! When I was a child, we used to pick violets and give them to our mother in little bunches. She had a pretty yellow eggcup — the last of a set — and she'd put the violets in that. But they weren't big like these, nor so velvety. These must have come all the way from France!"

"They did," he said. "I saw them in the window of Marchand's."

"You're extravagant."

"I thought of you."

(She was touched and flattered, and yet, a tiny, disloyal part of herself wanted to shout out, "There are gorgeous flowers for sale on every street corner in this city. Gorgeous *indigenous* flowers." But that wasn't fair. Neither she nor Philip were indigenous. Perhaps the violets were the right thing after all. Why was she so irritable with him? She reached out her hand again.)

"Philip, put the tray on the floor and come back to bed."

Suddenly, she had such a desire to hold him and tell him how much she cared about him and how grateful she was to him for rescuing her from —.

She always slept naked, but this morning, she had put on a loose cotton robe to sit up and have tea. Now, she took it off.

"Come back to bed," she said again. "I'll make another pot of tea."

Both the wives of Philip's co-workers and the market women seemed to think it strange that she had her sandals made in the market and often wore a piece of cloth, a *pagne*, as it was called here, wrapped around her for a skirt. Early on in her stay, she found this the most comfortable and modest garment for her walks around the city. In the market, she wrapped the cloth around her awkwardly and the women, laughing, had shown her where to start so that she would end up with her legs in two separate sections of the cloth. Now, she could walk freely and not be hobbled by the length or straightness of the skirt. She was not really trying to be African — she was too intelligent and self-conscious for that — and she never wore her long skirts in England, except perhaps to a party or at home. And she knew that many of the bold and brilliant designs that were favoured by the Senegalese (portraits of Senghor or current football heroes, wax prints in bright oranges and greens and purples) did not suit her skin or colouring, so she chose the more subdued patterns and colours, or bargained for the lovely indigo tie-dye cloth. Philip did not really disapprove of this — not in so many words. But he wasn't too happy about her wandering away from the Plateau. If she *must* go, he urged her to take Hyacinth, their steward, with her. But the steward did not like her — he had been with Philip and his first wife ("Wifie One," as she and Philip referred to her) in Abidjan; Philip, when he transferred, arranged to bring the man with him. He was devoted to Philip and not at all pleased when his master came back from overseas with a new, young wife. And Rona discovered that she was not good at giving orders. The English seemed to have a knack for giving orders; so did the French. Perhaps a sense of empire still lurked way down, deep in their subconscious. It didn't help, either, that Hyacinth was a man and that he was older than she was. "Would you mind?" she would say. "S'il vous plaît?" And whatever it was that she requested probably would not get done.

"Put the tray on the floor," she said. She liked making love on Sunday mornings, while it was still cool and fresh, and Hyacinth wasn't in the kitchen chopping up fruit salad for their breakfast. The city was quiet, too — or quieter, for Dakar was never really still. She liked that sense of Sunday mornings, and the privacy and coolness. She took off her robe and pushed the sheet down with her legs. "Come and let me thank you properly."

("I don't want to go and see Jennifer's baby," she thought, standing in the lukewarm sea and staring absentmindedly at the graceful dug-out canoes which moved slowly across the horizon. "I don't want to go back to England and have a child in an English hospital, away from my husband, and bring it back to turn over to a nurse girl, and then, send back to England at the age of seven, or ten at the very latest." There wasn't a European child on the beach who was over the age of ten. Yet, these were all excuses. She could modify or even change the conventions. She didn't have to have a nurse girl or go back to England to deliver her child. What was she *really* afraid of? To whom was she complaining in that fretful tone?)

She felt confined on the Plateau, with its broad avenues and plane trees, its shops run by Europeans, catering to European tastes. She felt that she had somehow jumped from youth into middle-age, without going through—what? Something indefinable, something that she sensed, but for which there was no name. Occasionally, she would see a young couple, packs on their backs, moving about the city, or sharing bread and cheese on a bench. Afterwards, the names of the streets seemed to mock her—Place de l'Indépendance, Boulevard de la Libération.

Philip was a cryptographer for the Foreign Office. He had a taste of Africa during the war and yearned to come back. Sitting in St. James's Park in London, or in coffee shops during those first few hectic weeks together, she sat as Desdemona must have sat with Othello and listened to Philip's stories about Gibraltar, Malta, Morocco, the Ivory Coast, and Senegal, where he was now living.

Standing in the water, knowing that she should have something on her head if she was going to stand like that much longer, it came to her that perhaps she had married Africa and not Philip. She turned and looked back at the beach. There was a whole group of people under the Avis' umbrella now. Mrs. Avis usually brought an enormous thermos of gin and orange and held informal court on Sunday mornings under the big umbrella. Today—as it was getting towards December—they were probably discussing how many turkeys could be smuggled in, in the diplomatic pouches.

The women sat around her on woven straw prayermats, not on the side with the mosque, of course; there was no need to be offensive. The mats were just the thing for the burning sands of the beach. The women thought that Rona was peculiar because she didn't come to their coffee mornings and she had been married five years without presenting Philip with a child. It was a good life for the women out here—or so it appeared on the surface. Yet a phrase of Oscar Wilde's (or somebody from that era) came back to her as she looked at them: "And as for living, our servants will do it for us." Released from housework and cooking and childcare, they seemed lost somehow, aimless. Perhaps the slaves felt like that after emancipation. They were good common-sensical women, not much given (unlike their French counterparts) to "style" and witty conversation. Their talk was mostly about servants, or their faraway children, or what they would do on leave. Rona found them incredibly boring, even the younger ones like Jennifer Phelps (she had bought Jennifer's new baby a small ivory bracelet for a teething ring. Philip pointed out that it would have to be thoroughly disinfected and that she was not to be hurt if, even then, Jennifer didn't use it). Most of the wives had been knitting matinee coats or embroidering their *batiste* nightgowns for weeks. The baby was now three months old—he had to stay in England until he was old enough to have a smallpox shot.

"Actually," Philip said, "John Phelps was in Marchand's buying a special bouquet for Jennifer. He called out to me and that's how I happened to see the violets in the window." They were now sitting in their robes in the cool dining room. Rona put a spoonful of paw-paw in her mouth and waited for the inevitable gentle question.

"Darling girl, why don't you go off the pill for a while? Just for a few months and let's see what happens."

The two paunchy young men over there. It must have been one of them. Their pale puffy bellies hung down over their bathing trunks, like bread that had been left to rise and then forgotten. She knew one of them—or knew who he was—an

American from Maryland. He also did de-coding. She had seen him and his wife at a few parties. "Rivah." Of course. It had to be him. She heard him talking once. His wife had been explaining to someone that she always kept the money when they went out. "They think Mastah's got the monah and Ah've reallah got it—it reallah fakes 'em out." "Sure do," her husband said in confirmation. "It surely does just that." It was the same voice that had said "rivah" and "Timbuktu."

She saw Philip swimming way out; he was an excellent swimmer, very slow and methodical, and beautiful to watch. He would be a little while yet. She began a sidestroke that would bring her just a little ways above where the two fat young men sat in a rubber dinghy, talking, each with a beer can in his hand.

"Excuse me," she would say, "did one of you mention Timbuktu?"


The train for Bamako left on Tuesdays and Fridays. She had not been able to find out much about the boat. The two men had their tickets arranged through a friend in Mali. She carefully found out what boat they would be on, for she was determined not to travel with them. They had not been pleased when she approached them. Reluctantly, they gave her what information they had. Perhaps they were afraid of what their wives might think. They were "gonna do a little huntin' in Mali as well," they said. She saw them back in Maryland, driving dusty trucks with gun racks in the back, and maybe big plastic dice dangling from the rearview mirror. Gettin' drunk on Sat'day night at the Legion. It was hard to imagine that these coarse men were working in the American Embassy. Perhaps they were good at their jobs—perhaps code work was more mechanical than she imagined it. It probably beat spreading manure and praying for rain. They weren't exactly *unfriendly* to her, but clearly they thought that she would cramp their style. Been out in Vietnam, perhaps, and picked up French and a taste for the exotic. Went back and married the girl next door, or the girl from the same district anyway; but the dreary monotony of farm life no longer appealed. Out here, it was always summertime and the livin' was easy. She thanked them and swam away. That night, she told Philip that she wanted to go to Timbuktu and they had the first real quarrel of their marriage.

"I can't get away just now," he said uneasily. (Jennifer Phelps had been plumply radiant with Jamie asleep in her arms.)

"Alone," she said. "I want to go alone."

"You can't do that!"

"Why not?" And she added angrily, "I'm neither a child nor a fool."

"What about your job?" She taught French twice a week at the American Embassy School.

"I can arrange for a substitute."

"Why Timbuktu?" he finally said, exasperated and worried.

"I don't know," she answered truthfully. "I don't know anything about the place, really. Its name means something to me, even though I never knew where it was, exactly, until I looked at the atlas this afternoon."

Philip turned his wedding ring around and around with his long, brown fingers. It was an unconscious and very moving gesture.

"I realize that you haven't been completely happy here," he said, looking at her with his uncanny blue eyes. "Sometimes, I even think that I was wrong to ask you to marry me and come away with me." She opened her mouth (to say what?), but he smiled and shook his head. "Let me finish." (Round and round went the gold band on his thin brown finger.) "You were very young when I met you and had just been through a bad time." (How she wept in his arms! How comforting it felt to let go! How surprised they both were when, in response to his innocent question, "How did you happen to end up teaching school in Birmingham?" she promptly burst into tears.) "We had both been through a bad time." (Round and round.) "I fell madly in love with you, you know—with your openness, your intelligence, your wit. You seemed so different from...from any other woman that I'd ever known. I think that I used Africa as a kind of bait—the way a rich man will sometimes use his money to get the woman he wants." Again, she opened her mouth, and again, he motioned her to be quiet. But she could not keep still.

110

"I love you!" she cried, "I love *you*! Surely, you know that by now?"

He nodded. "I know that. But you don't love this life."

She shook her head, her eyes full of tears.

"I don't know what I want—I just know that I have to get away for a bit. Right away."

"Why not Paris, then?" he said, brightening. "What about two weeks in Paris? Perhaps I can even get compassionate leave. If we told them that you had to see a specialist—"

"Why would I go to Paris and not London?" she said reasonably. "And anyway, I want to go to Timbuktu and I want to go alone. I don't feel real any more. I don't feel as though I'm a separate person. It's as though there were some limb or set of muscles that I'm not using, that I can feel shrivelling up, atrophying. If I don't go now, I'm afraid that I'll never be able to go anywhere alone again. I'll end up like those women who run off to the Hotel Croix de Sud as soon as their husbands go on trek. Eating their meals in the restaurant. Looking fearfully over the balconies. Afraid to go anywhere alone. "Please, Philip," she said, "please understand."

He managed a smile. "I'll try."

So, here she was leaning out a window, as the train slowly pulled away from the throngs of people on the station platform. Philip became smaller and smaller and smaller—a tall lean figure, standing out amid the crowds of Africans. The corridors were jammed with people leaning out the windows in spite of the warnings—"Défense de se pencher au dehors de la fenêtre"—posted on the wall. As the train curved slightly, she could see two white children being held up to look and wave goodbye to someone. She reflected almost immediately that they must be new to this country, for their faces were plump and rosy. They did not have the lean, pale, leggy look of children on their second or third tour. They were two cars up. She really should go and see who their parents were. (Yet, she knew that she wouldn't, for she did not want to get involved with anyone, in any way—it was necessary that she be alone.) As the train picked up speed, she went and sat down on her narrow bed. The fans were not working yet and the tiny room was like an oven. She had seen the man in the next compartment take out a prayermat and calmly kneel down, his face turned to the East. Even on a train, he did not forget his duty to God and to Muhammed.

Later on, in spite of her excitement and the violent swaying of the train, she fell asleep with the compartment door open. When she woke up, she saw that the man in the next compartment was facing the other way. The train had changed direction. A very devout man; perhaps he was going to pray all the way to Bamako. She did not know a great deal about Islam or the Muslims, although she knew a little bit more, now, about Timbuktu.

Maureen Avis had given her a bag of apples, three Mars bars and a warning to lock her compartment door. "Rape," she said. And she added, "Don't smile at me, my girl, it's happened." She ate a Mars bar and drank some of her store of bottled water, then she leaned out the forbidden window, into the night. Africans moved constantly to and fro along the cars—gusts of laughter and excited talk blew back in her face, like smoke. It was completely dark out and the moon hung as yellow as butter in the indigo sky. She felt tremendously free, speeding through the night like this, to Timbuktu. Well, not actually to the mysterious city itself, but to the Niger at least. She saw herself in her small cabin, waking up to the sounds of the river, going out on deck to watch the mists rise into the clear blue sky. She had not yet seen an African river, but she imagined it broad and muddy and full of crocodiles. Too much Humphrey Bogart. She smiled at her romanticism.

She and Philip had walked one Sunday to the Muslim cemetery, its gravestones all turned east towards Mecca. How simple life must be for a True Believer. There were things that you did and things that you didn't do. She had been several times to the Grand Mosque on the Allée Coursin and had visited the small women's mosque on the side of it. From what little she had seen, it was not a very good religion for women; but then, what religion was? When the train passed near a village or a compound, she could see the glow of charcoal fires and oil lamps. How strange the people in that village would find her—a white woman travelling alone, with no other purpose than to get up

112

the Niger to Timbuktu.

"There's nothing to see," Richard Avis warned her. He had flown up there a few years ago. "Oh, there's a nice Sudanese mosque, but precious little else."

Rona smiled sweetly at him. "I expect that you're right," she said.

Philip told her that Richard had suggested they take a few weeks' leave and have a holiday. There were planes to almost anywhere from Dakar.

"He thinks that I'm bushed," she said, pleased that she knew the lingo.

Philip smiled. "I expect so."

"Do *you* understand, Phil? *Do* you?"

"I'm trying."

How could she help but love him? Tonight there was a big dinner party at the American Embassy. All the diplomatic and British Council people would be going. She could have put her journey off until Friday — what difference would a few days make when one was going to Timbuktu? — yet, in the end, she couldn't do it, even though she suspected that her husband would not show up without her. Her bad self wished that he would go and fall madly in love with someone else. Wifie One had walked out on him and gone back to England — she hated Africa and she asked him to choose. Back to Sussex and muted colours, muted emotions — everything safe. Rona met several men who had been out here for years without their wives. Once-handsome men who drank too much and who were always in-vited to parties. Men who went home on leave and who had African "girlfriends" — and sometimes, African children as well. Yet neither husband nor wife divorced one another. The wife had respectability, a regular allowance, and a husband who only "bothered" her for six weeks out of the year. The husband had the prestige that he would not have enjoyed in his own country, plus his personal freedom. So long as there was no scandal, no real "occular proof" of what was going on, everyone turned a blind eye to the "girlfriends." But Philip's wife divorced him as soon as she could. He gave her grounds and did not contest the action. He said that he felt that he had let her down. "As he feels he has done to me."

The train had a wonderful horn — almost like an English hunting horn — a long clear note that raced along beside them for a bit, then fell away. A nervous young Frenchman came and stood beside her for a while. He was a linguist with some foundation and he was going to Mali to study the Tuareg people. He wore a short-sleeve shirt and she could see that his arm was still swollen from his shots. At one point, he went off and came back with two cold bottles of orange juice. "Jus d'or," she said. "En français, c'est très beau, n'est-ce pas?" He told her that there were some other Americans ("Je suis Canadienne." "Bien sûr," he replied impatiently) on the train, the parents of the two little girls — "Ils sont religieux" — and a man who was travelling by himself. They were all in his car, but only the single man spoke French. Very good French.

"Pas comme moi," she said, smiling and sucking on her juice of gold. She felt as though she were sucking on the cool orange moon.

"Ah, non! Vous parlez très bien." The pungent smell of his French cigarettes filled the corridor. A man whom she had loved, a man who had loved her and left her after she had crossed an ocean to be near him — he had smoked Gauloises as well. Then, she thought it was exciting that her hair and skin and clothes always smelled so continental. He had written her a letter in the middle of the night — or maybe written it long before — and had got up and left it for her on the kitchen table, propped against *The Concise Oxford Dictionary of the English Language.* "Dear Rona, I've looked and looked, but there is no nice way of saying this."

They had a tiny flat, above a jeweller's on Goodge Street. She was twenty years old and desperately in love. The gas stove ("the cooker") took pennies and only a certain amount at one time, so how could she be sure if she stuck her head in the oven? In the end, she fled to the grime of Birmingham and Bishop Ryder's Church of England Infant and Junior Schools — such a grand name for such a shabby, slummy place. One little girl had nineteen brothers and sisters: "Dear Miss, please excuse our Ethel becuz she had to stay home and help with the new baby." After a while, she found that because she was now working in England, she often had no sense of being there. She got up, ate a hasty breakfast, stood on the corner outside the fish and chip shop and waited for the bus to Five Ways. There, she jumped on another bus which took her down into the old heart of the town. Then, she began to walk. She realized that this was how England must appear to the English—and this came as a revelation. She was not a tourist any longer. "Ta-ra, Miss. Ta-ra." The shabby children ran out of the schoolyard to play in the shabby streets. She put her lover behind her, except sometimes in dreams, and began to enjoy herself. She went to museums, to the art gallery, to the newsreel theatre. She even took an occasional trip to London without too much pain.

(The young man threw his cigarette out the window and the sparks flew out like fireflies, into the dark blue night. He gave her his card and the address where he was staying and went back to his own car. The smell of his cigarette lingered for a long time in the narrow corridor.)

Philip insisted that she wire ahead to the Grand Hotel and make a reservation, if only for one night. She did not want to do anything so formal, but he pointed out to her that sometimes the train was as much as two days late and that she might be very tired by the time she got to Bamako. In fact, the train was only a few hours late, but it arrived after midnight and the moon was covered with clouds. She was glad, then, of Philip's advice, and followed a porter, with a large white "2" stenciled on his shirt, to a waiting taxi. Just as she drove away, she glimpsed, for an instant, the other white people who had been on the train. They got into the taxi behind her. One of the little girls was sobbing fretfully, like a child who has been awakened from a deep sleep and forced into its clothes. She heard the soft girlish voice of the mother—"There, now, there now, hush"—before she drove away. But she was too tired to speculate, too tired to do anything but stagger up the imitation marble staircase, behind the night clerk, whom she had to shake and shake before he would wake up. He was obviously contemptuous of her because she had insisted upon a room

115

without air conditioning, *non-climatisée*. It was not because these rooms were cheaper, but because she hated the chill artificiality of air conditioning. She preferred rooms with the old-fashioned three-bladed fans, where the change in temperature between inside and outside was not so extreme. Philip agreed with her, thank God. The flat that they lived in was fashionable, but old; air conditioning was put in only at the tenant's request. The young clerk muttered something under his breath as he opened the door to the room. The louvred windows were shut and the place was stifling and airless. Never mind. She gave him a nice tip and shut the door. Having adjusted the louvres and given herself a hasty wash (she would shower and wash her hair in the morning), she gave a little guilty, loving thought to Philip, far away in Dakar, maybe lying awake and thinking of her, and then stretched out, blissfully—alone, alone, alone. It took her a few minutes to get to sleep, for her body was still swaying from the motion of the train, but it was only a few minutes—for wasn't she young and wasn't she healthy and wasn't she almost on her way up the river to Timbuktu? Ou-Ou-Ou. Erotic and beckoning. She did not dream—or not in words and pictures. But every now and then, she seemed to hear the curious note of the train's horn, clear and golden, racing through the night. Jus d'or.

In the morning, she took her passport over to the *Sûreté*, where she surrendered it reluctantly, but she was assured that she would get it back when she was ready to leave the country. It was the first time in years that she had been without her passport and she felt vaguely uneasy. At the bank, she had a long wait before she could change her money into Mali francs, so the sun was already climbing swiftly to the centre of the sky (she saw the sun as some spectator in a cosmic amphitheatre, climbing higher and higher and higher, until he reached the very top row of seats) by the time she reached the office of the steamship company. There, she had her first real disappointment, for unless she wanted to go on the boat which was leaving tomorrow—the boat that the two American men would be on—there were no more cabins at all. Not for the next boat, or the next, and glancing at the Air Afrique calendar on his desk, after that, Madame, it was January and the river was drying up and who knows—

116

there might not be another boat until the rains. She bit her lip and wondered what would happen if she gave him a bribe — un p'tit cadeau. This was a funny country: there were armed guards at the border and you had to surrender your passport. Perhaps she would be arrested for trying to bribe an official. The steam-ship line was government-owned. She stood there, uncertain, trying to decide what to do.

"You can go, of course, as a deck passenger, Madame. Like the Africans. But with your skin, I personally do not advise it." Little blue plastic streamers blew from the fan on his desk. Could she do that? Could she live on the deck, under the burning sun, sipping bottles of lukewarm Evian water ("Si claire, si légère"), existing on ground nuts and fruit. It was a romantic idea — it smacked of Lawrence of Arabia. Have a heavy, body-shrouding caftan made here in Bamako; find a shop where they sold inflatable air mattresses. Salt tablets. She already had with her malaria medicine and enterovioform and halazone tablets, if she should run out of mineral water.

"Je reviens," she said to the official behind the desk. "I will return."

"If Madame wishes to embark tomorrow — ?"

"No. Not tomorrow. But perhaps as deck passenger on le bateau prochain. Je reviens."

The heat of the day assaulted her as she turned left and absently made her way back towards the cathedral. She had seen a little café there, with glass-topped tables set out on a shaded verandah. She was very hungry and thirsty; she would eat there. She was surprised that, in this most African city — far more African than Dakar, from what little she had seen of it — the café was run by Vietnamese. There were Vietnamese in Dakar, of course, for Dakar was part of the great colonial system of French-speaking people, who moved along that system from as far away as Indochina; but it startled her here. She sat down and gave her order to the bent old woman who shuffled over. And then, in front of the railing, which set off the café from the street, there appeared a plethora of beggars and boys selling airmail envelopes, mosquito coils, lengths of beautiful cloth, ballpoint pens and leather pendants.

117

"Eh, Madame!" "Eh, Madame!"

She opened her Michelin map and ignored them. How long would it take to get up the Niger? What if she decided to go on from Timbuktu to Niamey? Her stomach twisted with excitement, and when her food came, she couldn't eat it. She sipped instead on her *citron pressé*. She felt happy and free—after Niamey, she would possibly go into Nigeria and all the way down to the Niger Delta and the sea—and yet, Philip, or the fact of Philip, was there at the same time—a pull in another direction; a pull not so much of mystery, as of love. When they were first together, he bought her a copy of John Donne's poems:

*She's all States, and all Princes I;*

She loved him, she really loved him, and she thought that she understood, now, just what loving meant. Yet, at the same time, passing the public letter writers setting up shop in front of the post office, fresh from a good night's sleep (alone) and a delicious (solitary) breakfast, she almost stopped and asked the boy to write out a message: "Dear Philip, there is no nice way of saying this." "Dear Philip, I love you, but I'm bored, bored, bored with the people who surround you." "Dear Philip, it is not so much Timbuktu I'm after, but myself." "Dear Philip." "My dear husband." "My dearest friend."

She sucked at her drink and wondered if she could get a freighter back from Nigeria to Dakar.

"Well, you'll have to eat *something*, Muffie, or you'll get sick." Rona swung her head around. Just a few tables away sat the American woman and the little girls from the train. The mother and her daughters had on dresses that were made of the same material and almost the same style. The children had on white sunbonnets as well. Two men stood in the doorway which led to the dim interior of the restaurant proper, discussing something; the older man was doing all the talking with the old Vietnamese woman who had served Rona her lunch. She could not hear what they were saying, but the younger man seemed agitated—he folded and unfolded a piece of paper in his hands—and the older man looked tired and a little cross. At one point, he said something quite sharply to the old woman, gesturing at the table, and the young man shook his head and put a restraining hand on the older man's arm. Rona tried not to stare. She was afraid to move her chair to a more comfortable position (from which she would be able to look at them without craning her neck) for fear that it would scrape on the concrete floor. She watched curiously as a small child of perhaps eight or nine came slowly up the stone steps of the verandah, leading an old woman. The child's dress was clean, but it was torn and faded and Rona could see that the old woman was blind. River blindness, probably. She had read about it. She had read that sometimes a single child will lead a long line of men and women blinded by the river, lead them from village to village, begging. The couple moved slowly from table to table, but few people looked up to drop a coin in the empty jam tin that she held out to them. Gradually, they worked their way to the side of the verandah on which Rona and the American woman were sitting. (The two men were still engaged with the old Vietnamese.) The child looked at the two American children sitting in their new, bright cotton dresses. She looked at the American woman and she held out her tin.

"Madame, un p'tit cadeau. Pitié de nous, Madame. Pitié de nous."

"What's she saying?" the older child asked in her high-piping voice.

"What's she want?"

The mother's voice seemed less soft, less childlike now.

"She's begging. That old lady's blind."

"What's she begging for?"

"She wants us to give her some money."

"Does she want all of us to give her some money? What's she going to do with all that money?" The child's voice was fretful, puzzled.

The African girl stood there, impassive, holding out her tin.

"Tell her to go away," the little girl said. "Tell her that she's not supposed to beg. Tell her what the book says, Mommy."

"Go away," she said. "Shoo. Go away."

The girl didn't move. The old woman began a kind of high-

119

pitched chant, almost a whine.

"Pitié de nous," the girl said again, but without emotion or appeal, the way someone might say, absentmindedly, "Pass me the salt, will you?" or to a hovering waiter, "Two beer."

"Go away," the small girl shrilled. "Go away."

The customers on the verandah stopped talking and were watching the little drama (if one could call it that) between the impassive African child and the white woman. For a few seconds, the only sound (and part of Rona's consciousness, used to the noise of the African cities by now, thought how incredibly quiet it was, all of a sudden) was the high-pitched chanting of the shapeless old woman, whose skin hung from her bones like a hand-me-down suit of clothes. Then the older of the two Americans, perhaps noticing the strange un-African stillness on the verandah, wheeled around and seemed to take in the situation at a glance. There was a clink of coins and the African child, jam tin on her head, leading the old grandmother, went slowly back the way that she had come. The hubbub of voices began again. Rona turned back to her map, oddly shaken. It was not the begging that had upset her. The opaque eyeballs of the old woman were nothing compared to the twisted and rotten limbs of the lepers. (At first, they terrified her. Most were Muslims and crawled, or limped, or hobbled after her in their long white robes, sticking their claw-like hands in her face, persisting, persisting, persisting. It was as though the sweet diseased breath of Africa blew over them, as gales blew over the palm trees down by the shore, knocking off branches, twisting limbs, bending some of them to the ground. Nothing in her upbringing or education had prepared her for the lepers.) No, it was the determined, almost hysterical manner of the mother and her oldest child. Terrified self-righteousness, that's what it was. The Frenchman on the train had said that they were missionaries. The eldest child had a missionary voice. "Tell her that she mustn't beg." Rona ordered another *citron pressé*, and again, bent over her map. She saw Philip holding out his love for her, not begging —the English didn't beg—but holding it out, saying to her, "Pitié de moi."

"Deux bières," the American shouted, and sat down across

from her without asking.

"Thank Christ, *that's* settled," he said as though they were old friends, he and she, "or should I say, 'Thank Abdu'l, Baha'." He looked so good-humoured, and at the same time, so fed-up that she had to smile.

"Where are your friends?"

"Packed 'em off to the hotel for a sleep. I couldn't stand it any more. The kids are cranky anyway. It'll do them good."

"Are you travelling together?" she asked.

"God, no. Do I look like a religious nut to you?" He had on a brown straw hat, with a hatband made of a strip of local weaving, in the black and white geometric designs much favoured in French West Africa. He took off his hat and wiped his forehead with a large white cotton handkerchief. The old woman brought him his beer and bowed to him with respect.

"She's a religious maniac too," he said, grinning at Rona. "Would you believe it?"

"What religion?" Rona asked, trying to imagine.

"B'hai," he said.

"I've heard of it, but I don't really know anything about it."

"Good. Neither do I—or not much. Just what the Weavers told me on the train." He had already started on his second beer, giving a deep sigh of satisfaction.

"God, I love African beer! How I'll ever be able to drink that American piss again, I don't know." He wiped his mouth. "Try some of those pickles. They're delicious. Everything here is delicious. It's not a bad religion, actually, or it doesn't seem to be. Preaches universal brotherhood, the end of war, you know the kind of thing. From what I can understand, it began as a breakaway Islamic sect. Now, or so the Weavers say, it's all over the world, and even has a universal court, sort of like the World Court at the Hague. And probably equally as effective," he added.

"Had you met them before last Tuesday?"

"How do you know that I met them last Tuesday?"

"I was on the same train."

"You were!" He looked at her with renewed interest. "How come I didn't see you?"

"I didn't see you either, but someone described you—and the Weavers—to me."

"Well, isn't that a shame? We could have got drunk together. I'm P.J. Jones," he said, shooting out his hand. "I'm pleased—very pleased, I might add—to meet you."

"Rona Hooper," she said, extending her own hand. "Are you staying here long?"

"Hey, the man's supposed to ask that question!" And he laughed because he made her blush. "I'm only kidding. Strangers in a strange land, as the saying goes. Things have to be established. Yes and no to your question. Here in Mali, yes. Here in Bamako, yes and no. I come and go."

"Go where?"

"To Timbuktu."

She didn't believe him. He had seen the red circle on her map.

"You're teasing me."

"Not at all. Perhaps I should go on with my introduction. After all, if we'd met at a party, and liking my looks from across the room, you had rushed over to your hostess and said, 'Who is that attractive, large—You would say large, wouldn't you, not fat? (Rona nodded)—man over there in the corner?' you would have meant, not just what's his name, but what does he do? Right?"

"I wish that I could say 'wrong'."

"Well, she would say, 'That's P.J. Jones. His mother named him Pliny, but he can't stand the name, so you'd better not ask what the 'P' is for. And he's the engineer who is widening the airstrip at Timbuktu.... Wherever that is,' she might add."

"And is that really what you're doing?"

"That is really what I was hired to do and what I've been doing and will continue to do, when I'm not running around acting as interpreter for a family of innocents who come out here without knowing any French or anybody, except they have a letter from some Vietnamese contact, written in pidgin, whose last name is the same as at least ninety percent of the Vietnamese population of West Africa."

"Does the old woman know who it is?"

"No. And the contact had promised to find them a house. But

I knew that she was a B'hai—so, I brought them here. She maintains that she knew nothing about their coming, but they do have the letter, so it can't really be a mistake. Anyway, she's a good old bird and I think that she'll help them. They're to come back tomorrow afternoon at four."

"The woman seemed really angry about the beggar girl."

"B'hai's aren't supposed to beg. It's also a religion with a strong work ethic. She was offended, she said. D'you know, they hadn't been west of New Jersey in the States—come from around Trenton, I think they said. And they get on a plane after saving and working for three years, and wham, eight hours later, they're in Dakar and boarding the train for Mali."

"They must have really deep convictions."

"Really deep something. They don't, either of them, speak a word of French, and none of them has had a cholera or a yellow fever shot. Now, the littlest kid is feeling really sick, because, of course, they weren't allowed out of the airport until *that* little oversight was corrected. Nobody checked them when they got on the plane." He smiled at her.

"Is all this boring you? I felt that I had to talk to someone or explode. I had to find them a hotel room and take them around to the *Sûreté* and the bank this morning, and then, come here with them this afternoon—and now, the first day of my week off is all fucked up, if you'll excuse my French."

Rona began to fold her map carefully, getting all the creases right. P.J. was nice, but she wanted to be by herself and think about what she should do. How strange it was that he was working up at Timbuktu. She wondered if that would be a good thing, or bad. He seemed nice and friendly and more intelligent than he let on. Also married. He wore a broad band of African gold on his ring finger.

"I must go," she said.

"That's not fair! Now you know everything about me and all I know is your name. Can't you stay and chat a little longer? Or better still, how about dinner tonight? Where are you staying?"

"At the Grand Hotel."

"Well, so am I. And so, temporarily, are the Weavers. But we don't have to eat at the hotel. I know a very pretty place called the Lido. We can sit outside under the African moon."

"I don't know, I—"

"What don't you know?" He lost his bantering manner.

"I'm married," she said. "Very happily married."

"I see." He paused, then he regained his grin. "But, my dear young lady, I'm only asking you out to dinner. And I'm old enough, I think, to be your father."

("So is he," she wanted to say. "He's old enough to be my father, too.")

"All right. What time shall I be ready?"

"Around seven-thirty. I'll order in advance, shall I, things that I know that they do well?"

"That sounds nice. I'll be down in the lobby at seven-thirty."

He made no suggestion that he go with her now and she liked that, although she could feel his eyes on her as she walked away. As soon as she was around the corner, she searched out a cab and asked the driver to take her to the swimming baths. And while she swam, she thought to herself, over and over, "Will I? Won't I?" and sometimes, "Should I?" On her way home, she stopped and bought a postcard of a Mali trader and wrote on the back of it: "Dearest Philip, I do miss you" and gave it to the hotel clerk to mail. Then, she went up the marble staircase, to rest a little before it was time for dinner.

Leaning over the staircase to see if P.J. Jones was down there, for she didn't much like the idea of sitting in the lobby alone, she saw him deep in conversation with the young man whom she now knew to be Mr. Weaver. She was wearing one of her long skirts, one that she was particularly fond of, not a tie-dye, but a subdued wax print in a dull yellow and brown, and a brown scoop-neck T-shirt that she had bought the last time that she and Philip were on leave. P.J. looked up as she approached.

"You're lovely," he said, standing up. "All you need are some amber beads. Perhaps we can find some for you. Bamako is a good place to pick them up." The other man also rose and stood there smiling shyly at her. He was very thin and pale and his Adam's apple stuck out so much that, except for his pallor, it really looked as though he was bound to choke to death at any minute.

"Rona Hooper, meet Joe Weaver. Rona is from—where did you say you were from?"

"I'm living in Dakar," she said, holding out her hand. The three of them sat down. She wondered if they were going to dine with the Weavers—if they were going to wait until Mrs. Weaver and the little girls came down. Suddenly, she felt irritated at herself. Two nights away from home and she needed a man to protect her. She should be wandering around the streets by herself, finding some little place that caught her fancy, not going to a meal that had been ordered in advance by someone else.

Philip had reached up and grabbed her hand, just before the train pulled out. "If you need me, I'll come," he said—and that irritated her too. Need him for what? She had been in West Africa for five years now and she knew the *lingua franca*. Women were respected in this part of Africa, not harassed. This wasn't Turkey or Spain or Mexico; women had power here—and status. So what was she doing with these two Americans, sitting sipping martinis in the lobby of the Grand Hotel?

"Are you staying long?" the young man said. His Adam's apple moved up and down. She remembered the old songs at the newsreel cinema in Birmingham: "Just follow the bouncing ball." She tried staring at his left ear.

"I'm not sure. I'm just having a little holiday." One felt that this young man would not know a holiday if he saw one.

"I saw your wife and children at the Vietnamese café this afternoon."

"Ah, yes! Madame Thieu has been real nice to us. She's going to find us a place to live."

"And then—?" She could have bit her tongue.

"And then?" The young man looked puzzled.

"What are you planning to do after you find a place to live?"

"Why, whatever needs to be done. Whatever," he said in a firmer voice, "God's will tells us to do."

P.J. drained his glass. "We made reservations, so I think we had better get going."

125

The young man seemed almost frantic at this announcement.

"You'll be all right," the older man said, "the menu here is in English as well as French." He went over to the desk and said something to the clerk. Rona thought that she saw some money change hands. "Oui, monsieur," the clerk said loudly. "Oui, monsieur, bien sûr, certainement." P.J. nodded, then he came back and extended his arm to her.

"Shall we?"

"Will they be all right?" she asked as they went out the door.

"No, of course not. They think that the food's too hot and that the streets are too dusty and that the beggars are too persistent, and Christ knows what else! But they see their duty and they are here to do it. In an awful way, I can't help admiring them, even though I find them naïve and ill-informed and a general pain in the ass."

"What can you admire in them, then?"

They had decided to walk to the Lido; P.J. said that it wasn't very far. "Oh, a kind of romantic vision, I guess. I don't have it or I wouldn't be widening the airstrip at Timbuktu. Think of all the tourists that will bring in. And Timbuktu itself is just a sad dusty town. Maybe it still means something to the Arabic world, but it won't mean much to the tourists. Mind that drain," he said pulling her away just in time.

Over coffee (thick, sweet Arab coffee), she told him about her plans.

"I wondered what you were doing with that map."

"I don't understand it myself. I stood up in the water and heard this voice mention Timbuktu. All of a sudden, I knew that was where I wanted to go."

"I keep telling you, there's nothing there."

"Well, maybe I just want the trip along the river."

"Maybe." He took a sip of his coffee and gave her a searching look.

"What do you mean?"

"Doesn't your husband care if you wander around West Africa by yourself?"

"Being picked up by strange U.N. types?"

"You could do worse," he said.

"I'm not looking for a man," she said. "I told you, I love my husband very much."

"What are you after then?"

"I don't know. A sense of my own reality—my separate reality. In order to stay with him, perhaps I have to prove that I still enjoy doing things by myself." She laughed nervously. "Does that make any sense?"

P.J. reached over and took her hand. "You're too pretty to be so wise."

"Don't," she said.

"Don't what?"

"Don't make remarks like that. It spoils everything."

"But you *are* pretty."

"Maybe. But couldn't I still be wise?"

"Of course."

But he withdrew his hand and called for the cheque. "L'addition, s'il vous plaît."

They wandered around the city. He showed her where to buy delicious loaves of French *pain* and where to get the best brochettes of beef or chicken. It was fun walking through the African night with him. Although he tended to play the caricature American, she could see that he loved Mali and loved his job. He had to learn the language in order to train his second-in-command, who would eventually take over from him. He had been designing bridges when the opportunity for this job came up. He still wasn't sure, in terms of Malian culture, whether the bigger airstrip would be a blessing or a curse. He had been here eighteen months so far and it was going to be hard to leave.

"What does your wife think of all this?" she said, parodying him, as they sat at a café of the hotel having a final drink.

"Oh, she stays in New York and likes her life there. I miss her sometimes. She's a photographer, quite a well-known one. I admire her tremendously."

Rona wished she could say, "I'm a something. Not just, I'm a wife." She wished that she could ask, "Do you love her? If so, how can you bear to be apart?" But, she went on sipping at her drink, long after the drink was gone and the ice cubes had nearly melted.

"I think that kind of innocence is dangerous," she said suddenly. P.J. seemed nearly asleep.

"What?"

"The kind of innocence that the Weavers have."

"What harm can they do?"

"They have pre-judged everything, and also, they put everything in God's hands. Or whatever *His* name is. Since there is no such creature, everybody ends up running around and taking care of them."

"You sound jealous," he said. She was surprised at the prickling in her eyes.

"Oh, maybe. But, not really. I don't want to be taken care of —by God or anyone else. I want to take care of myself."

"Sometimes, it's blessed to receive."

(She saw Philip holding out his love, his empty tin, "Un p'tit cadeau, pitié de moi.")

"Sometimes."

He yawned. "I have to get up early tomorrow. Get some work done before I take the Weavers over to the café."

"I've really enjoyed myself," she said. "Now I've got to go back to my room and sleep on my decision."

"You're really going to try it?"

"Why not? The next boat doesn't sail for a week. I can explore Bamako and get a caftan made, wander around a little bit."

"Don't do it," he said.

"Why not?"

"I'm not convinced you're 'going to.' I think that you're 'running from'."

She smiled and shook her head. "No. That's exactly what I'm not doing."

P.J. cleared his throat. "Do you want to come to bed with me?" he asked. "You're awful pretty and I've really enjoyed myself tonight."

"No," she said, touched. "But thank you."

"No harm in trying?"

"None at all."

And so, they kissed each other's cheeks and went down the corridor in opposite directions. Once again, she didn't dream and fell, this time, immediately into a deep, refreshing sleep. Tomorrow, she would *really* decide—tomorrow.

But she did not see P.J. Jones all day and she found herself somewhat disappointed. She went back to the steamship company and said that she would sail as a deck passenger on the next boat up the Niger. Then, she went into the market and ordered a caftan made out of heavy woven cloth, and also, a pair of loose trousers.

At noon, she was at the Vietnamese café. The same African girl came by, leading the same old woman. It was a repeat of yesterday in many ways, but she liked sitting there and looking out at the crowds. Bamako wasn't divided like Dakar. It was a black town, an African town, and in spite of the heat, she found it exhilarating. The fact that she did not have her passport no longer seemed to bother her. Perhaps she would not need it ever again. Perhaps she would go up the river and down the river and simply disappear. A new life. Without ties. Without love that chained her, that made her a slave to her emotions. Leaning on the bridge in the late afternoon, she saw her life, spread before her, as distant and magic as the mysterious veiled kingdom of Timbuktu. As changeable as the great river itself. Nobody married forever any more. Commitments were like manacles.

"Dear Philip, there is no nice way of saying this." But she missed him today, really missed him, and she sent him another postcard, this time of the graceful pirogues which plied the river.

"Dear Philip, I miss you. Am going up the river soon. Will call before I go."


She was lying down on her bed, quite at ease now that she had made her decision, when somebody knocked on the door.

"Who is it?"

"P.J. Open up."

"Wait a minute."

She put on her robe and opened the door. She had been half-asleep and was annoyed at this interruption.

"What's the matter?"

"The Weavers' littlest child is quite sick with fever. D'you think you could babysit her while we go to see about a house?"

"Babysit!"

"C'mon, Rona. It's no skin off your nose. We'll be back in an hour. I want to get a doctor too."

"I'll have to get dressed—."

"Room 220. Thanks a lot." And he was gone.

She walked slowly down the corridor, her anger mounting. Why should she babysit these kids? She had come here to be alone, and already, she was in the midst of a whole complex circle of relationships. But when she saw the children, she forgot her anger. The older one was sitting by her little sister, whose rosy cheeks had taken on a hectic, unhealthy flush. "There now," the little girl said in her mother's voice, "there now, hush."

"Hello," Rona said. "I've come to stay with you until your Mommy and Daddy come back."

"That's nice," the child said, as though she had been expecting her.

"Muffin's really sick," she explained, "I have to keep cold cloths on her forehead. That's what my Mother said."

"I'll help," Rona said. "Why don't you play for a while?"

"All right," the child said obediently. She rummaged in a little suitcase and came up with a colouring book and some crayons. "I'm very good at colouring," she said, "I always keep between the lines." It was a B'hai colouring book, but it reminded Rona of the simplistic pages that she used to colour at her own Sunday school. Jesus Blesses the Children. Jesus with the Fishermen. Always happy—or positive—scenes. Never, Jesus on the Cross or Mary Weeping.

Rona was worried about the sick child and lay on the bed beside her.

"What's your name?" she said to the other sister.

"I'm Janet and she's Muffie—Margaret really—but nobody calls her that. We came on an airplane," she confided. "Mommy was crying."

"Why? Was she sad to leave her friends?"

"I don't know. Daddy told her it was God's will." The child carefully selected a colour. "D'you think Muffie will die?"

130

"Of course not! What a strange idea! She's got a very bad reaction to her shot."

"If she dies and we bury her out here, she'll be all alone when we go back home to Trenton."

"She isn't going to die."

"She'll do what God wants her to," Janet said. "It's out of her hands."

Rona found this aphorism, coming from the mouth of a child, almost obscene. On the bedside table by the sick child was a jug of water and a book, *Baha'u'llah and the New Era.* She leafed through it, sitting on the bed by the sleeping child. There was an almost Germanic profusion of capital letters: "He, His, Servant of the Blessed Perfection, Declaration, Supreme Singleness, the Most Great Peace." But, as P.J. said, the basic tenets of the faith were harmless, indeed inarguable "motherhood issues," one might say. B'hai. How exotic it sounded! Like *The Rubaiyat of Omar Khayyam.* But also, sheep-like. Baa-Baa-Baa. She learned that a B'hai accepts his lot with "Radiant Acquiescence." The Weavers didn't seem very radiant. There were a lot of old-fashioned Biblical endings on the verbs: "enacteth, enforceth, sitteth, cometh, shineth." She shut the book and put it back on the table.

"How's your colouring getting on?" she asked the little girl.

"Okay. When are my Mommy and Daddy coming back?"

"Pretty soon. Are you thirsty? I could ring down and get the boy to bring up some Coca-Cola. Would you like that?"

"Yes, thank you." The child did not look up from her work.

"I don't know how to talk to children," Rona thought. "Or not this child. She's like a little old lady, a little old self-righteous spinster lady." As if to confirm this, when she put down the phone, the child said, "It is forbidden to drink intoxicating liquors."

"It's not forbidden to *me*," Rona said sharply. Yet this remark would not have bothered her coming from the mouth of a Muslim. Perhaps she couldn't accept B'hai, simply because it was a religion that was new — or newer than Christianity or Islam? People had probably felt the same about Luther. "Self-righteous bastard" and so on. Anyway, the child was only repeating what she had been taught.

There was a knock on the door.

"There's our drinks," she said and she fished in her purse for some change. But when she opened the door, it was the Weavers and P.J. Mrs. Weaver was being supported by the two men and she was moaning and sobbing. For the first time, the little girl's unnatural composure broke and she ran to her mother, clinging to her skirt and looking up at her with wide, terrified eyes. P.J. shook his head and gave Rona a wry smile.

"We've had a little trouble." They half-carried, half-dragged the young woman to the empty bed and lay her on it.

"Ruthie," her husband said, "we're home now. It's going to be all right." This sent the woman off into a fresh paroxysm of weeping.

"Home!" she wailed. "I want to go home!" The sick child awoke at the sound of her mother's wailing and she began to cry as well.

"What happened?" Rona said. "What's the matter? Did she fall?"

"Well, it's nothing to get alarmed about," the young man said. "Ruthie's just had a little shock."

"He wouldn't let go," the woman wailed. "He put it on me and he wouldn't take it off."

"Was she *raped*?" Rona whispered. She couldn't imagine it.

"No, no." The young man blushed scarlet. "P.J. and I were sent to look at a house where we might be able to stay and Ruthie went off to find a drugstore. What d'you call it here?"

"A *pharmacie*."

"Yes. Well, she went off to find a 'farmassee' and we said that we'd meet her back at the café, and if the place was okay, then we'd come back here and pack up."

"So?"

"So, the place was real nice. A whole group of B'hai people living together in a big old house. We can move in anytime. One of 'em even speaks some English."

"No!" the woman screamed. She sat up, eyes wild and teeth chattering. "No! We're going home! We're going back to Trenton! I'm not staying here another day!"

132

The young man made an effort to ignore her. "She'll be all right. It's so new to her, you see. She got kinda frightened."

"I've called a doctor for both of them," P.J. said. "He'll be along any minute."

"But what *happened* to her?"

"As far as we can make out, she got a bit lost and while she was standing there trying to decide which way to go, a group of beggars came after her."

"Beggars?"

"Lepers."

"Oh God!"

The husband took up the story.

"You gotta understand—as I said, Ruthie's never travelled very much, neither of us have—and she's newer to the faith than I am. Begging is forbidden to B'hai's. So is giving of alms, unless to other B'hai's, and out of the common treasury. And she'd never seen people like that before, no hands or legs, and faces rotting away. Jabbering at her in French. They wouldn't let go of her and one old guy, from what she says, sort of put his stump on her arm and wouldn't take it off."

The young woman lay back on the pillows, moaning.

"We went looking for her when she didn't show up at the café," P.J. said. "And then, we saw her running along a street with all these lepers coming after her, and she was screaming at them that they were devils and filthy and so on."

"Lepers are very frightening," Rona said, "very frightening and very persistent. After five years, they still scare me."

"I'm not attaching any *blame*," he said, "I'm just telling you what happened."

"She says that she wants to go home," the young man said. "She says that she won't stay here and she and the children are going home." Big tears rolled down his cheeks. "She has to stay. It won't be the same without her."

This time, the knock on the door was the grinning desk clerk with drinks, and the doctor. Rona donated her gin and tonic to P.J., who looked as though he needed it more than she did. Then, she excused herself and walked back to her room. Ruth, she thought: "Whither thou goest I will go." Women had been

133

following men around for centuries, maybe since the beginning of time. She was very depressed and found that she couldn't sleep. She got dressed again and went out into the streets, confused and sad. She bought Philip another postcard, a Tuareg and his camel. "République du Mali. Tombouctou. Les fidèles compagnons." The camel and his master posed proudly under a blue untroubled sky.

"There's nothing up there any more," P.J. had told her. "Just a dusty crumbling town." Yet once, scholars gathered there to study and decipher the mysteries of their faith. Once, small boys had been put in chains for not knowing the whole of the Koran, while the kings' daughters walked proud and beautiful, and unveiled, through the busy streets:

> *She's all States, and all Princes I;*
> *Nothing else is.*

A companion was, literally, someone with whom you broke bread. She had been a faithful companion to Philip. She looked at the ring through the camel's lip and the rope which hung down from it. His master's hand was not in the picture, but you knew that he was holding the rope. They needed one another, the Tuareg and his camel. What a handsome man the Tuareg was with his black beard and flashing smile! He wore a little leather charm around his neck to keep away the evil spirits. She knew that she should go back to the hotel and see what she could do to help the Weavers. If she had been surrounded by lepers on her fourth day in Africa, she, too, might have become terrified and hysterical. And she had travelled. She had worked in the slums of England and combed nits out of dirty little heads, passed by the school for the "dummies" every day on her way to Bishop Ryder's. The dummies, with their big heads and coarse features, had stared at her through the fence. Sometimes, they called out to her in their thick voices. She used to dream about them at night. And out here, she had got used to cockroaches and lizards scampering into the corners of cupboards and bureau drawers. Got used to. Accepted. But leprosy was a word with as many connotations as Timbuktu. Coming from a small town near

134

Trenton, New Jersey, what could prepare one for the lepers? Perhaps Ruth saw their deformities as somehow a result of their begging, rather than the other way around. The wages of sin. She looked absently at the stalls along the roadside. Little tables covered with old watches, old keys, ceramic beads, Nescafé or its Malian equivalent, "Brun d'or." Her bare toes were dusty from the red earth. Tomorrow, she must get together a really good medical kit. Plenty of salt tablets, bandaids—everything that she could think of. The Niger lay out there, as old as Africa itself, a broad highway of adventure and self-discovery. She saw a display of pretty little strings of market beads and bought a few for Janet and her little sister.

When she got back to the lobby, P.J. was sitting in a big armchair, drinking.

"How are they?"

"The little girl's all right. The doctor gave her something for the fever. I'm not so sure about the mother. She's had a sedative and is sleeping now.."

"And Joe and Janet?"

"I had some sandwiches sent up. He's upset, but he's determined to stay. Apparently, the whole B'hai community got together and paid the balance of their fares. One way. They haven't got much money. He's a carpenter and figures that he can get work." He sighed. "I really don't know. I seem to get involved with the weirdest people. Present company excepted, of course."

She sat down opposite him.

"You're going to give them the money, aren't you—if they want to go back?"

"Oh, he won't go back. He's just not the kind of person who could renege on his duty to God."

"But the woman and the children?"

"Yes, I suppose so."

"You've already offered it."

He smiled at her. "You think that you're pretty smart. Well, what if I have? I expect she'll calm down. But you and I both know that Africa isn't for everybody—and maybe, if she knows there is a way out, she'll be more likely to stay."

"Timbuktu," Rona murmured.

"What?"

"Nothing. I must go up."

"Have you eaten?"

"Not yet."

"Would you eat with me again or would you be bored?" He paused. "I've had a call and have to fly back up tomorrow, instead of next Monday. It can be a kind of farewell party—or *au revoir*, if we run across each other in Timbuktu."

"All right. Where shall we go?"

"Leave it to me."


It was late when they returned to the hotel. After dinner, he took her for a ride on the river. She felt peaceful again, peaceful and sure of what she was doing. The only thing missing, she thought, was a crescent moon in the sky.

"Thank you," she said. "I've had a lovely time."

"I don't suppose," he said, "that you'd care to fly up with me? You could go on by boat from there. Those American fellows that you told me about would have got off."

"No. But what a generous offer."

"You're sure? No strings attached."

"I'm sure."

In the night, she heard a knock on the door. She held her breath and pretended to be asleep. The person knocked again and went off down the hall. She wanted Philip's arms around her; she wanted Philip *and* her freedom. How could she have both? She tossed and turned and thought that the morning would never come.


As she went out (late, so that P.J. would already have left), the desk clerk called to her.

"Madame! Your fren' have left you somthin."

He held out a small brown paper parcel and leaned over the

desk, grinning, while she opened it. Inside was a string of heavy amber beads, the colour of dark honey. She put the beads on.

"Eh, Madame? Ça vous va bien!" Smooth and golden as the words of the Prophet himself. There was no written message — nothing.

As she left the hotel, she happened to glance up at the Weavers' window. The louvres were shut tight, although it was nearly noon. She paused for a minute, then realized what had caused her to look up. In the room behind the window, she could hear Ruth Weaver's plaintive wail, over and over, "I want to go home, I want to go home, I want to go ho — ."

Rona sighed and walked back into the hotel. She didn't know what she would say. She didn't even know whose side, if any, she was on. "Téléphonez le médecin," she said to the boy at the desk. "Vite. Hurry up." Then, she ran up the marble staircase. The amber beads, like love, hung beautiful and heavy around her neck

"You go to the people who need you," P.J. said to her last night. "You go to the people who need you."

That was all very well, but he was in Timbuktu.

## DÉJEUNER SUR L'HERBE

They travelled together as brother and sister and even made a
game of it, volunteering this "fact," if it did not somehow come up
naturally in conversation; but the truth of the matter was that
they were old (and Platonic) friends. Once, years ago, at a time
when both of them were still married, they had gone to bed
together and ended up laughing. They knew too much about
each other, even then, to start a romance. He knew all about her
stretch marks and deep depressions; she knew all about the zinc
ointment that he used for his haemorrhoids and his not being
allowed, at age thirteen, to attend his mother's funeral. There
was no mystery. And her husband was his close friend; the bed
that they had "gone to bed" in was the large comfortable bed
that her husband, who was clever with his hands, had built.
Eventually, both marriages broke up, for reasons that had
nothing to do with the "going to bed": he left his wife; five
years later, her husband left her. There were periods when they
saw very little of one another; he moved to a different part of the
city, miles away, and he had a series of live-in girlfriends, all
much younger than he was (his wife had taken the children and
gone back to Halifax, where she was born). Sometimes, when he
was a little bit drunk, he would say things like, "When my wife
left," and it would make her furious, for he had forced her to

leave. She thought that he was a show-off and a hypocrite; and his passion for girls who were at least fifteen years younger than he was, amused and affronted her. He thought that she was a neurotic, judgmental bitch, who treated her husband, his friend, as though he were a cross between her father and the hired hand.

Yet somehow, they always came back together, wrote letters, talked on the telephone, met each other for a meal or a drink. One night, when they were both quite drunk, he told her that he would never desert her and she looked at him and knew that it was true.

Last autumn, after her latest lover left, she called Robert on the telephone long distance (she was teaching in another city at the time) and told him, bravely, that she had started saving money to go to France. He heard what she was really saying, for often she had a child's way of dealing with the world, indirectly, through insinuation. "I don't suppose that you'd be interested in going with me?"

He'd been a bit drunk when she called, having just lived through another unholy row with his girlfriend.

"Bon voyage," he said. "This fish ain't biting."

But a few days later, sitting at the kitchen table, utterly exhausted by yet another scene, he picked up the telephone.

"All right," he said. "You're on. I haven't got a dime, but we'll figure it out."

She went downtown the next day and made airplane reservations for two, bought a Michelin guide and a Berlitz *French for Travellers,* and mailed them off to him.

"Thank you," she wrote. She did not tell him how desperate she had been feeling when the phone rang, how she had been standing in the bathroom, naked, staring at the medicine cabinet and wondering whether or not she should get dressed and go for help. When she was in the bookstore, she looked in the Berlitz book under "doctor."

"I've got a pain here."

"How long have you had this pain?"

She felt like one of those queens in the fairytales, who have to get a certain thing to eat or drink or they will die. Only, what she wanted was love; to be loved. Her latest lover told her that

140

she was "too independent." Her husband told her that she "leaned on him" too much.

"I have had this pain," she told the imaginary doctor, "all my life."

"Ôtez votre pantalon et votre slip, s'il vous plaît."

"Please remove your trousers and your underpants."

Friends sometimes asked her if, really—tell the truth now—weren't she and Robert lovers?

"No," she said, "that would be incest." And she added, "Besides, *I'm* over twenty-five!" But she knew that there was more to it than that.


In spite of the many small economies, standing at the bar rather than sitting at a table if they stopped somewhere to have a drink, treating the ubiquitous *pâtisserie* windows as gorgeous still lifes (all on the general theme of sweetness), rather than as invitations to enter and buy; in spite of the *Résidence Lutèce*, where the morning coffee tasted of chicory, and the *douche* cost extra and was two floors up, Paris was proving to be more expensive than their worst imaginings. So, they always carried their lunch with them when they went out for the day—a *baguette* or two, sausage, a piece of cheese, a tomato, and of course, a bottle of cheap wine (although, even there, the price was no longer *ordinaire*).

They eyed longingly the fruits and vegetables at the *primeur's* next door: the thick white asparagus with its pale purple tip, the fennel, the aubergines! It would be lovely to have a little flat where they could cook. Next time—if either or both of them ever came back. And they wanted to come back, both of them. They loved Paris; they loved it all! Except for the litter in the streets (but London was like that—and New York and Montreal) and the incredible prices (but there again—London, New York), they found little with which to quarrel. One evening, sitting side by side, in one of the *vedettes* which took sightseers up and down the Seine, watching the slow spread of the sunset, learning the names and histories of the bridges (her favourite was the Pont Neuf; his, the Pont Royal), they confessed to each other that

Paris had turned out to be as beautiful and as charming as they had hoped.

"Sometimes," she said, "I build up such high expectations of a place that I am bound to be disappointed when I see it. But Paris *feels* the way I wanted it to. It feels like my dream Paris."

"Did you walk so much or so far in your dream Paris?"

"Maybe not. I suppose that I rode in taxicabs and carriages; but I don't mind the walking, I really don't. Maybe I'll even lose some weight."

"You ought to do that," he said. "Seriously. I can't understand how you could let yourself get so fat. You're really a very attractive woman — or were."

"I don't think that I want to be attractive anymore," she said. "I think that I've had it up to here with being 'attractive'."

"Then do it for your own sake," he said. "You're too young to be so overweight and middle-aged. I worry about you."

"Thanks," she said, and she turned away from him, staring out over the water. She thought, "How cruel he is to me! Why can't he leave me alone?"

He had fallen in love again, between the buying of the tickets and their actual departure, and had admitted on the plane to London that he nearly hadn't come. His new girl had just moved in with him and he was uneasy and distressed at leaving her. This time, it seemed like the real thing. He said that he was surprised at himself, at how much in love he was. "God, I love that woman!" he would say as they walked the streets or chatted over lunch. And she would look at him with her cynical smile and say, "So you keep telling me." Robert's girls never got any older, or rather, the ratio of years between him and them stayed pretty much the same. When she teased him, he told her, quite seriously, that she did not understand "the aesthetics of the flesh."

"I suppose not. I do understand, however, that line in *Beautiful Losers*: 'When I was sixteen, I stopped fucking faces'."

But he confessed, also, while they moved slowly under the bridges, that he really was enjoying the trip, that he was loving it.

They spent a few days in London first, where the time change made them wide awake at 4:30 a.m., and so, they got up and dressed and walked and talked, each morning, the streets almost totally deserted. They took pictures of each other on West-minster Bridge, listening to Big Ben strike 6 a.m. (Yet, when he told the story of their early walks to a distant cousin who had taken them out to dinner, he said, "I knew Marguerite was also awake, because she wasn't snoring." Cruel! He was always cut-ting her down! When she defended herself in front of the cousin, by pointing out that he snored too, he said, "Oh yes, but it doesn't bother you.")

Everywhere, there were warning signs about unattended parcels:

*DON'T TOUCH*
*DON'T GET INVOLVED*

and whom to notify.


There was a picture of Margaret Thatcher in the papers, at-tending the memorial service for the M.P. who was blown up. In Victoria Station, while she waited in a huge crowd and Robert went off to check that they were in the correct line for the boat train, she suddenly noticed a small case, like a child's suitcase, off to one side. She did not know the right thing to do. Robert was coming towards her; he was so tall that she could see his head above the crowd. Did she call out, "Robert, there's a bomb!" Did she go and stand in front of it? Could she get to a guard before it went off? Then, a mother, dragging a crying child, came along and scooped up the parcel. It was not a bomb at all—of course not. She was so afraid that she thought that she was going to be sick. How could people live with such possibil-ities? It seemed to her that, all her life, she had been lacking some sort of insulating material that kept other people from feeling things so deeply. Her mouth had already opened for the calling of Robert's name when the woman with the child came hurrying up. The M.P. had survived World War II, only to be blown up when he started his car. She remembered being hit in the back of the head with a snowball when she was young. The snowball had a lump of coal in it and it hurt terribly, even through her toque. And the shock of it, the outrage. Did the M.P. have time to feel that stunned anger before he died?

In spite of the morning walks, and the pubs and plays, she was glad to get out of London. One night, walking in Soho, there had been two young men in thick boots, bashing each other with bits of pipe. And all the sex shops. *Rubber* magazine, the models advertising leather and bondage. At the National Gallery, her handbag was examined; his briefcase. Cruelty and suspicion were everywhere. "Don't Touch. Don't Get Involved."

In conversation with another friend, male, he had once said, several years ago, that no woman could really give you the orgasm that you got from jacking off. She objected.

"If that's all you really want!" she said. "Surely, there's more to it than that? Being held, cuddled; the other body which is always, even when people have been together for years, a mystery." To her surprise, his friend had agreed with her. He had always seemed, to her, even more callous than Robert. She had been very sad that night, missing her husband, and her children who were spending a year with him. Robert phoned and she asked him to come over. He brought his friend, whose name she could not remember, and two bottles of wine. After the first bottle of wine, she asked if they would wash her hair for her — it was very long and thick — and she knelt on a chair at the kitchen sink, while they took turns pouring warm water over her head. Then, they took turns drying her hair with towels and kissed her and went away. Later, the friend — Peter? Paul? — sent her a poem about that night and washing her hair; and she was very touched. But she also remembered how they laughed about some woman that they had both fucked. They liked to go downtown and watch strippers, inviting them back to the table for a drink.

At the *Résidence Lutèce*, the patronne was surprised that they wanted two beds. It was so much more expensive. You could see from her face that she was interested in them and wondered what their history was, if there had been a quarrel. They explained that they were brother and sister on a long-awaited holiday. Ah, how charming—and, of course, they must have two beds! They were on the fifth floor, facing the street, where they could hear the constant sound of the traffic down the rue Monge, and the hee-haw of the ambulances. They had tall windows that opened in, and a small, beautifully-wrought ironwork safety railing. They came in at night, after a leisurely meal and a long walk, and drank and talked, she, in her nightgown; he, in his dressing gown, at the small table by the window. They liked walking the city so much that they hardly ever took the Métro. Robert wore the star-shaped key to their room like a sheriff's badge, sticking out of his jacket pocket, on the way up and down to the desk. But he wore a *béret* and a soft woollen scarf, a present from the new girl, and he looked so continental that it was hard to believe that he was from Canada. He kept the map and the "kitty" and she was content, for the most part, merely to go wherever he suggested. The fights with her last lover had worn her out and she felt as though she were still convalescing from some awful illness. Robert said to her one day that something seemed to have gone out of her, some kind of necessary, absolutely fundamental energy. When she mentioned her lover, he told her to leave it alone, let it go. "I'm an impressionist myself," he said. "I deal with the moment and don't always look for the eternal aspect of things." Later, she saw a sundial in the Jardin des Plantes. It said: "I only count the happy hours." She resolved to do better.

But always, he was there with his little hammer, tapping away at her. "Why don't you lose weight?" "Why are you so bitter?" "Why do you always fall in love with losers?" When she came back from the Ladies Room in the swank restaurant in London, he was telling his cousin the history of his marriages and girlfriends. "Marilyn!" she said. "If he's only got to Marilyn, we might as well forget about the play!" For she had her little hammer too and she wasn't afraid to use it. But he just laughed and said, "You're just jealous because you haven't had as many husbands and boyfriends as I have had wives and girls." "*Jealous*," she said scornfully. "Jealous!" The cousin looked from one to the other of them with a puzzled smile.

But most of the time, they got on very well. He could always make her laugh, as well as make her cry. One Sunday, they walked to the Place des Vosges. The weather was stormy and the grey sky threatened behind a row of brick houses, pricked out the grey stone. The square was something of a disappointment; the statue of one of the Louis on his horse was poor, and the fountains, nondescript. But they had walked a long way and they decided to have lunch on a bench. It was May 27th, *La Fête des Mères*, and when a young woman, her blouse unbuttoned, strolled by carrying a bunch of roses in clear cellophane, Robert whispered, "See that? That's a whore taking flowers to her mother." A very sad-looking woman sat two benches over, smoking cigarettes. She smiled at their laughter and called out to them, "Bon appétit!" She probably thought that they were two lovers having a picnic. Because the woman looked so sad, Marguerite almost thought that she should go over and explain the situation. "Voyez, you see, we are only friends travelling as brother and sister. He never touches me."

Robert bought two large macaroons as a special Sunday treat, but as soon as he unwrapped them, a huge flock of pigeons descended on them, pushing for crumbs. One of the pigeons had a horrible growth on its neck, a kind of caul, and Robert, who was squeamish about such things, tried to shoo it away. It kept coming back, however, and they became hysterical with laughter, screaming at the pigeons in French and English, and flapping their arms. When the rain came, they ran for shelter, still laughing, across the square.

"Now," Marguerite thought, "now she will see that we are not real lovers or he would be kissing me in this doorway, licking the sweet crumbs from my lips."

They walked and walked—they bought postcards along the Seine and walked to the bird market, which bothered both of them, because of the cages—to the Tuileries, where the slender metal chairs, made to look like the delicate gilt chairs of far-off salons, had been left in groups which seemed, to them, to tell stories. It was raining that day, too, but very gently. They were the only people in the gardens and they took two of the chairs under a large tree, so that they could eat their lunch.

"That group," she said, "that is a father and mother, very respectable—see how their chairs face the path unflinchingly and directly—and their teenage daughter, who would rather be anywhere else, but who is too well brought-up to say so. See how the one chair is just slightly apart from the others?"

"That group," he said, "is a bunch of tourists, very noisy. They are taking pictures of everything, especially of one another in front of everything. I think they are German."

"Why do you think that?"

"I won't tell. Yes, they are German."

"That chair all by itself, under a tree. That is the lady's chair."

"And those two, facing each other..."

"The lovers, of course."

In the end, he took a series of photos of the chairs; they really were strangely eloquent. The whole day turned out to be lovely and they felt very close to one another.

"You're beginning to look better," he said and she squeezed his arm. "I wish that you were really my brother," she said, but that wasn't quite what she wished.

"Sartre est vivant!" was scrawled with red paint on a wall.

"Well," he said, "it would be nice to live 'across the park' or whatever it was they did, Sartre and Simone."

"Don't you ever want that?" she said. "Don't you ever want, as your companion, someone who is your intellectual equal?"

"Oh, I get enough of that anyway. And the women that I love aren't stupid, although you may think them so."

"I never said that."

"You don't have to." And she didn't pursue it, because it was such a lovely afternoon and they had been so close. It was as though she had put her hand in her pocket and felt her little hammer, and then, taken her hand away. For he had called them stupid himself, some of them anyway, the early ones, the ones just after his first wife, whom he had also called stupid. "You stupid cow!" Shouting at her, out on the front lawn, with his children standing together and watching it all, not really understanding, or maybe not even hearing the actual words, just the tone of contempt. Later, when her husband said such terrible things to her that she thought that she could never get over them, never walk down a street on a May afternoon and feel even a quiet sort of happiness, Robert said to her, as comfort, that she had to

147

understand that there was something called "the exaggeration of desperation," and the things said were all part of that. And she and Robert did it to one another, sometimes said terrible things. Was that the same though? If so, what were *they* desperate about? Each could leave; was free to leave at any time. It wasn't the same thing; it couldn't be.

As they came out of the Jeu de Paume, he said, "My God, we've seen a lot of painted flesh in the past few days!" So, as an antidote, they went and laughed at Napoleon's stuffed dog and looked at case after case of dress-up clothes that Frenchmen had worn for killing, the "officers and gentlemen." At what point did man begin to kill his fellow man? Was it over a bone, a cave, a woman? It began back in the water, perhaps, and was carried forward onto land. "Mine, it's mine, it's mine." And the women accepting it, or at least pretending to, even urging the men on. Napoleon's dog did not know that Napoleon was emperor, but he would have known who was master. In the end, they were sickened by all the uniforms and firearms, and hurried out into the sunshine. Her ex-lover had written to her that it had been a "battle" between them, and then added, "No, a war! *La lutte continue.*" Because he had been younger than she was, she thought that things would be easier, that there could be an equality between them, a "mutuality," but it had not worked out.

When a pretty French girl went by, Robert said, "Oh God, I'd like to fuck that one!"

"You'd like to go home and say you'd fucked a French girl?"

"Well, why not? What's wrong with that? It would be like drinking at their well."

(And everywhere there were the statues—"Mort pour la France"—as though it were the feminine that was, *au fond,* responsible for all the conquests, the cannonballs, the screams, the fountains of blood.)

At the restaurant, last night, there had been a stupid Englishman, in a party of six, who had asked to see their *sentier* map. She had it spread out on the table, as they were planning a walking tour in the valley of the Loire. In miniscule letters, above the French word for "beacon" on the map, she had written the word "markers." The Englishman was drunk. "What is this in your country?" he said. "What are snackers? Something sexy?"

"Such a stupid man," she said afterwards. "Such a stupid, stupid man."

Robert disagreed. "We can't be judgmental. That poor man had been cast as the life of the party."

"Do we have to play out roles that other people impose on us?"

"It's easier."

"Do you think women impose rules on men?"

"That's more complicated. Certain agreements are reached, especially in marriage; certain contracts are made."

(He had come in one night, years ago, after his marriage broke up, but hers was still intact. He had been to see a movie of *The Picture of Dorian Gray*. It had affected him in a curious way, as though he had only, just then, in the darkened movie theatre, become aware of his own mortality. "I want to fly!" he cried to them. And then, laughing at himself, "Before my feathers fall off!" A year later, he married a girl who was nineteen. His role, from then on, was always one of provider or protector, at least insofar as his wives, or the various women with whom he lived, were concerned. Yet, in the end, there would be fights and rebellions and pettiness and he would find somebody new.)

"Even the excitement of a new body in the bed," he told her once, "the aesthetics of the flesh." The women who did not love him hated him. It was about fifty-fifty each way. He brought his new girls to her for her approval—or disapproval, which amused him more—and often, months later, the girls would sit on her couch and sob. She never knew what to say.

In the phrase book:

> *I'm ill.*
> *I'm lost.*
> *I've lost my _____.*
> *Keep your hands to yourself.*
> *Leave me alone.*
> *Lie down.*
> *Listen to me.*
> *Stop or I'll scream.*

He had a way of making friends with anyone, anywhere. It came from a certain arrogance, a belief that he was always right. On their way back from the Place des Vosges, he stopped at a stall and bought flowers for Madame la Patronne of their pension. She had discovered their washing hanging over the bidet and the wash basin.

"Je vous en prie!" her note began. "Je vous en prie! Il est interdit..."

He gave her the flowers and told her, in his terrible accent, that she was the loveliest flower of all. She laughed and told him that he was foolish, but there were no more notes about the washing.

He came into her room at the hospital, the day after her third child was born. She was sharing with a young Italian girl and the whole family had been visiting. He stood in the doorway, laughing, carrying an enormous bunch of white and yellow daisies. "Well," he said, "have they found out who the father is yet?" He had the nurses scurrying for vases, and soon knew where the Italian family lived, shared the joy of their first grandson, etc. He seemed to know always just the right thing to do, as well as just how much he could get away with. But he had a dark side, too. ("You stupid cow." The young women sobbing on her couch.)

"Does it bother you," she said to him one night, as they sat in front of the high windows in their night clothes, drinking wine and looking down at the street, "Does it bother you that I've just been trailing along after you, letting you study the map, make all the decisions, just like the sort of woman that I've always despised? Following you around like a faithful dog?"

"No," he said, "that doesn't bother me. You're a good companion. What bothers me is that something seems to have died in you."

"What?" she said desperately. "What has died?"

"Oh, I don't know. Some self-love. Some necessary self-respect. You seem so old to me. You seem to have collapsed all of a sudden, to have stopped trying. You've let yourself go."

"And you?" she said. "What about *you*? What have you done with your life?"

"I'm happy," he said. "I enjoy my life."

"How can you? How *can* you?"

Later, she watched him as he walked to the corner to try and phone home. She pretended to be asleep when he came back, but he ignored her pretence.

"I did it! Only for a minute, but I could hear her as though she were next door."

She kept her eyes shut.

"Would it bother you," he said, "if I sat at the table and smoked my pipe for a while? I want to jot down a few things."

"No," she said, "it wouldn't bother me at all." And she turned on her side, away from him, where he was sitting at the window. She heard him open another bottle of wine and light his pipe.

"Oh God!" he said. "Oh God, I love that woman!"

And then, softly, "Marguerite, do you think I'm too hard on you?" but she didn't answer. She felt like an unattended parcel, ticking away in the corner of the room. If he touched her in any way, she would explode.

On their last day in Paris, they decided to visit Montmartre and Sacré-Coeur. The *Blue Guide* warned them not to; it put down the basilica as "only too visible from almost every part of Paris" and lamented the fact that hardly anything remained of old Montmartre. They wanted to go anyway, climb the steps and look out over the city. But they were late getting started and it was nearly noon by the time they got off the bus. They had planned to spend an hour just mooching around the streets before going up to Sacré-Coeur itself.

"I think that we should eat first," Robert said. "We're still a long ways away." It was getting hot as well and they both thought that they could do with a drink.

"Are there any parks around?" she asked. "Let's make it someplace nice for our last *déjeuner* in Paris."

He looked at the map. "What about the cemetery?"

They were standing in the middle of a bridge and they could see the cemetery, or part of it, below them. There were trees and paths; it might be pleasant.

"It's probably illegal, as well as a mortal sin," she said, "to picnic in a cemetery. We might get arrested and get our pictures in the paper: 'FOREIGN PIGS SHOW NO RESPECT FOR WAR DEAD'."

"I think that most of the war dead are somewhere else." He was looking in the *Guide*. "There seem to be a lot of famous people buried here."

She hesitated.

"Oh, come on," he said. "We're hungry and thirsty and we have a chance to picnic with Degas and Nijinsky. I'll take your photograph."

But once they got over the bridge, they could not find a way in. A wall seemed to run around the cemetery for miles, and they began to wonder if there was any public access at all. The sun was hot on their necks when they turned a corner onto a narrow street which reeked of dog shit. They had to be careful where they stepped.

"Christ," he said, "do you think all the dogs come here for the bones?"

And still the high brick wall was on their left side—and no entrance. A woman came walking along behind them, and then, in front, pulling a small boy by the arm.

"Rue Merde," she sniffed. "Rue Merde" and she warned the boy to watch where he was stepping. Robert and Marguerite began to laugh.

"Shall we give it up?" he asked. "I'm starving."

"Oh, we can't give up now, it's all too funny."

So, they went back to the bridge and started again, and this time, they found the entrance.

The cemetery was like a small town of narrow houses, with steep roofs. Most of the paths had names, like streets, and it was all very peaceful. They sat side by side on a stone bench and began their lunch, although, for propriety's sake, they kept the wine bottle in the carry-all.

"I feel as though we ought to pour a libation," he said. He looked at the *Guide* again and raised his glass. "Salut, vous fantômes vénérables!"

"It is impossible for me to believe," she said, "that it's all just snuffed out, at the end, like a candle."

"Yes, and that Yorick's skull probably looked just like Stendhal's, that Nijinsky's thigh bone could just be something for a dog to chew on."

He drank some more wine and then he took her hand. The gesture was so strange and intimate, coming from him, that she was terrified.

"Well," he said, "what on earth are we going to do about you?"

A woman in a flowered dress came up the path. She was carrying a kitten and talking to it, or to herself, it was hard to tell. She did not so much as glance at them as she passed by, and yet Marguerite withdrew her hand.

"I'll be all right." She leaned over to pour some more wine from the carry-all. "I'm just feeling unloved right now. It will pass. I'm enjoying this trip though. Thank you for coming with me."

He looked at her and shook his head. She laughed. "Oh, we'll probably ride off into the sunset together some day." And she laughed again. "On separate horses, of course. Like our *chambre avec deux lits.* Do you think that we could be buried that way, in the same grave, but in twin coffins, or in one of these mausoleums, side by side, in drawers?"

They began to take pictures, tipsy on the wine and the heat and the sense that they were doing something rather shocking. He posed on a large black gravestone, smoking his pipe; she leant against the iron grille of a mausoleum. He even went so far as to kiss a pretty angel. She took his picture while he kissed the angel and put his hand on her marble thigh.

"Watch out!" she said. "What if she wakes up?"

"What if I turn to stone instead?"

It was a strange game that they were playing, there in the cemetery, while the pigeons fluttered around the stone bench where they had eaten their lunch. "I love you," she wanted to say to him. "How can I love you so much and hate you so much all at the same time?"

They did not notice the woman coming back along the path,

still muttering, until she stopped in front of Robert, who had been absorbed in arranging Marguerite beside a wreath of artificial poppies. She said something unintelligible, then held out her hands to him, then went on.

Robert and Marguerite looked at one another.

"Where's the kitten?" she said. "Robert, where's the little kitten?"

"There's nothing that we can do," he said.

"But her hands were covered with dirt! We've got to do something. Suppose that it's still alive?"

"I think that's what she was trying to tell me," he said.

"What?"

"That the kitten was sick. That she killed it."

"Are you *sure*?"

"No, I'm not sure. But there really is nothing that we can do."

"Don't Touch!" Marguerite shouted at him. "Don't Get Involved!" He looked bewildered.

"What the hell are you talking about?"

But she was already running down the path. "I'm going to find that kitten. You made it up, about what the woman said!"

He grabbed the carry-all and camera and started after her. It would be easy to get lost in here. He was really angry with her now.

"And what if you do?" he called after her. "What then?"

## CROSSING THE RUBICON

Today is the ides of February, February 13th. I was actually looking up "idiot" in my Concise Oxford (*n*. Person so deficient in mind as to be permanently incapable of rational conduct; utter fool. f. Gk. *idiōtēs* private person, [*idios,* own, private]) when I noticed "ides" at the top of the page. I knew what it meant, of course, or thought I did; but as it is virtually impossible for me to stop with one word when consulting a dictionary, I read the definition anyway: "*n.pl.* (Rom. Ant.) Eighth day after nones (15th day of March, May, July, October; 13th of other months)." That surprised me. I had always assumed, because of Caesar, that the ides invariably fell on the 15th. And yet here it is today, by one of those strange coincidences, the ides of the month I am in. Another piece of trivia, I thought, to cram into my ragbag of a mind, where reside such useless bits of information as the Harvard telephone number of my first real boyfriend (Kirkland 7-1044), a man whom I have not seen or heard of in twenty-five years; or the day of the week on which my sister, then aged eleven, had her appendix out. And yet, yesterday, I couldn't remember where I put the car keys.

I am trying to write a story which I do not particularly want to write. But it nags at me, whines, rubs against the side of my leg, begs for attention. I won't be able to go on to anything else

155

until I deal with it. In this context, the fact that it is the ides of February seems ominous—"Beware, beware"—and I wonder if I might be better off doing something, anything, else.

Tomorrow is Valentine's Day and my daughter has announced that, when she comes home from school, she and her girlfriend, who has been invited to stay the night, are going to make Valentine cupcakes for all the boys in their class. This is really not much of a task: we live on an island and the total population of the school, boys and girls, is fifty-one. If they make cupcakes for all the boys in the top three classes, it will come to little more than a dozen.

"What are you going to make for the *girls*?" I call sarcastically. I am standing on the porch in my flannel nightdress and she is running down the path to catch the yellow school bus.

"Paper Valentines. Handmade. We can do that while the cakes are cooking."

I do not make any political comment; she is already out of ear-shot and what would be the use? Nothing ever really changes. The boys will accept the cupcakes as their due; the other girls will understand. That is the way it is in elementary school, even in the Enlightened Year of Our Lord 1980. In grade seven, my sister and her girlfriend, Shirley, held their first boy-girl party on Valentine's Day and they worked for hours on the food. This was partly to impress the other girls (it always is), but mostly to impress the boys. I remember that they borrowed a heart cutter from Shirley's mother's bridge-sandwich set and made two or three dozen heart-shaped egg salad or tuna fish sandwiches. My mother and I sat upstairs while the party was going on, eating all the "surrounds," as it were, and playing gin rummy. One of the naughtier boys fused the lights by putting a penny in the light socket and then screwing the light back in, and my mother got really mad when she found out what had happened. My father was out, so she had to go down the steep steps to the cellar, carrying a candle, and she was afraid of the dark. Later on, she gave my sister and Shirley a lecture on "promiscuity." (She had heard the squeals and giggles in the dark, oh yes.) I had never heard that word before, but listening outside my sister's bedroom door, I soon caught the drift of the conversation. My mother wanted to have a word with the boy's mother. My sister vowed that she would never go to school again, never ever, if my mother said even one word. Later on, I could hear the two girls giggling and re-living the party when they were supposed to be asleep.

I was in town the other day and bought a half-pound of candy hearts—the flat pastel ones with mottoes—and I expect that some of these, carefully chosen, will go on top of the cupcakes. They are just like the ones we used to buy when we were kids, although they don't seem to taste as nice. These leave a bitter taste, like candy-coated pills, if you suck on them too long. But the taste isn't the important thing, it's the mottoes. What surprised me was that most of the mottoes are the same as they were when I was a kid growing up in the forties. Because I don't want to begin my story, I have taken some of the hearts out of the glass jar, where we've been keeping them, and have shaken them onto the kitchen table (which is also my desk). I've turned them right side up. "TO EACH HIS OWN," "WHY NOT SAY YES," "BE GOOD TO ME," "LET'S GET TOGETHER," "KISS ME," "BE MY SUGAR DADDY." I pick up a pink "LOVE ME" and pop it in my mouth. It seems rather touching that these things are still sold in a big city like Vancouver, where the number one hit song recently was, "Good Girls Don't—But I Do." Good girls certainly didn't when I was growing up, only bad girls, girls from the East Side who hung around the lockers in the basement of the high school where the vocational boys hung out. They had loud, defiant laughs, these girls, and red lips, and their sweaters were too tight. (Or so it seemed to me, seeing them through my mother's eyes.) Everybody knew about them, of course, but nobody wrote songs about what was going on. And if a good girl got into trouble, she went to Arizona for a few months—for her asthma.

"YOU'RE A SLICK CHICK," says this one. Good heavens, where are these made? In some small town, by-passed by the Trans-Canada; in some equally obscure factory, where the women still wear snoods and current jargon never filters in? "SLICK CHICK," indeed! I must try to find out where these hearts come from. Do the workers in the candy factory still jitterbug in the staff canteen and listen to a skinny Frankie singing, "That Old Black Magic's Got Me in Its Spell?"

My story is set in Montreal and it will begin with a woman on a Number 24 bus, heading East along Sherbrooke Street. She is on her way to meet a man who used to be her lover. The bus passes a clock, and seeing that at this rate she will be early, she decides to get off at Peel and walk the rest of the way. They have arranged over the telephone to meet at Place Ville Marie at noon and go somewhere nice for lunch. She is staying with an old friend and when she wakes up, there is a note shoved under her door. "Ma belle, back soon. Will drive you anywhere." But she has decided that she does not want to talk this morning, even to her dear, dear friend, so she has dressed carefully, had a quick cup of coffee in the empty kitchen, and gone for a walk, until it is time to catch the bus. She likes being in Montreal again, likes the bilingual chatter, likes the business of the place, likes the little shopgirls and secretaries in their smart clothes. Vancouver, where she lives, is a veritable frontier town as far as *couture* is concerned. And she likes old things and old places — the patina that they have. Old people too. One of her very best friends is eighty-five. She has noticed, while still on the bus, a Hundertwasser exhibition at the art gallery. If things get too tense, she will tell him that she planned to go to that. The conference for which she is here does not officially begin until this evening.

"The boys are getting paper Valentines as well," my daughter calls from across the road, "the cupcakes will be extra." When I was at the candy counter in the Bay, I bought her a bag of solid chocolate hearts, which she does not know about, and upstairs, in Fabrics, enough heart-embroidered braid to make hairbands for her and her two best friends. Later, in a drugstore, I saw a button which said: "Cinderella married for money." I knew that she would find that funny, so I bought that too. Some of the buttons were very crude and I couldn't imagine who would wear them. Bad girls, I suppose. But maybe not. In Delhi, India, last year, a friend of mine saw an otherwise perfectly respectable-looking American girl walking along the Raj Path in a T-shirt depicting a drunken kitten holding a martini glass in its paw. Underneath was written in pink letters: "Happiness is a tight

158

pussy." How could even a bad girl wear a thing like that? How could she pick it out of the pile and hand it to the cashier? How could she wear it in India, let alone back home? Sometimes, I feel like old Miniver Cheevy in our high school literature books. "Born too late." How we laughed at *him* in grade nine!

He had fallen in love with her, and one afternoon, they had slept together. Then, he went home and told his wife. They called her up and asked her to come and see them, to talk, to try and untangle this thing. She couldn't go right then, she said, because she was alone in the house and her children were sleeping. She did not suggest that they, being childless and more mobile, should come and see her. She imagined tears and shouting, and coward-like, she did not want her children to be a witness to all that. The next day, his wife came to see her. "If it had been a girl off the streets," she said, "I could have dealt with it better. But *you*. I can't compete against you."

She wanted to say, "Oh, my dear, it's not a competition," but it was. It always, to some degree, is.

"It won't happen again," she said. "I think that he's just feeling restless and unsure."

"I feel as though I've been walking around in a bubble for the last six years," his wife said, "and now, it's burst."

So, the woman in my story will get off at Peel, one fine October morning, and walk down to and along St. Catherine's. The last time she has seen him was at Dorval Airport, six months before. The night before that, the three of them had gone to hear Charlebois at Place des Arts, a farewell treat for her. She dressed carefully that night too, and when his wife put on her old down jacket over her dress, he suggested that she might wear her good coat instead. "It's *cold*," his wife said stubbornly. "It's still *cold* out there at night." She knew that he was comparing the two of them and that he wanted them equally dressed-up.

"Leave her alone," she said. "My vanity will probably cost me pneumonia."

He sat in the middle, as usual, and when Charlebois sang, "Pourquoi vas-tu si loin?" she wanted to touch his knee, but she didn't dare. All that was over. It had been over for a long, long time. The next day, when he missed the turn-off to the airport and they ended up in a dreary suburb before he could turn around, his wife said from the back seat, laughing, "You see, he doesn't want you to go." It was all right if *she* said it, so they all laughed.

In grade three, we graduated from pencils to pens with steel nibs. They fitted into long wooden holders that were lacquered in bright primary colours. We wiped the points with felt pen-wipers that we made during art lessons the first week. Penwipers are as obsolete as ice-picks now, I guess. The sharp steel nibs were wonderful for carving names and initials into wooden desks. If you were caught "desecrating the furniture" (I can still hear the voice of Mrs. Albee, my 3B teacher), you were sent to the principal to be paddled. The paddle hung on a hook behind the principal's desk and had "BOARD OF EDUCATION" stencilled across it. I don't believe that it was ever really used on the girls (he had easier ways to make us cry), but I remember many a boy returning red-faced and defiant, easing himself care-fully into his seat. The boys were very naughty. They held our heads down in the drinking fountains, dipped our braids in the inkwells, tied our dresses to the backs of our seats, put rubber dog turds at the door of the girls' cloakroom. They made us cry. Still, secretly and carefully, we carved their initials and names into our desks: "AC + SF," "JM + PM"—Tom or Dick or Harry. Then, we stuck a finger in the inkwell and rubbed over the new incision, to make it look old. We were always covered in ink, all of us, for one reason or another. Now, my daughter comes home with letters and initials up and down her arms. She stands at the sink, scrubbing them off with the nailbrush, because she wants to wear a short-sleeved shirt tomorrow. And the littlest girls stand in the schoolyard with their skipping ropes, chanting the same old rhymes:

> *FIRST COMES LOVE,*
> *THEN COMES MARRIAGE,*
> *THEN COMES BABY IN THE*
> *BAY-BY CARRIAGE*

160

(Yet well over half the kids in that school have parents who are single or married again). Faster and faster, they skip, until the boys jump in and spoil it all.

"I don't know why I like him," my daughter says to me about the predominant set of initials. "He's not *nice*. There are lots of boys much nicer than he is."

"Niceness doesn't seem to have much to do with it," I tell her. (He should probably get a "HIT THE ROAD" on the top of *his* cupcake, but I'll bet you a dollar, it will be a "LOVE ME.")

She sees him before he sees her. He is sitting by the fountain, dressed in the old English policeman's cape that they found one day in an antique shop. She has a cape as well and she is glad that she didn't bring it. They are made of real felt, lovely and warm, and belonged to the Eastbourne Constabulary of maybe fifty years ago. She smiles to think that he has worn it today.

He has not seen her; she can still leave. Once he turns around and looks in her direction, she will be hooked. All he will have to do, then, is reel her in. My mouth hurts, just thinking about it. I cannot give her such a painful metaphor; I will have to think up something else. Right now, I want to play soothsayer and call out to her, "Beware, beware. Walk away. Run. Leave well enough alone. You're cured." She stands there at the edge of the huge square, hesitating. He turns, sees her and waves.

It was so nice that they could all be friends. Everybody said so, although a few people — mostly women — told her privately that, really, they couldn't understand how his wife could bear to have her around. After all that had happened; after all that she'd been through. "Maybe I'm a kind of reminder," she would say smiling, sipping her drink. "Something like a *memento mori*. I can't remember my high school Latin, but let's say a *memento perditi,* a 'remember you could lose him again.' But that's pretty cynical. I actually think that we like one another. When he's not around, we have a lot of fun together, go to galleries and window-shop, go out to tea. After all, he's made his choice, we all know that. It might be more to the point to ask why *I* put up with it, but frankly, I don't think that I could give you an answer."

"And when the three of you are together?"

"We have a fairly good time. We tend to talk too much and

we tease him a lot—back one another up, because we both know him so well. He protests, but actually, he loves it."

"Did you really all live together?"

"Briefly."

This was where she usually changed the subject or got up to find another drink. If she were feeling bitter or witty, or both, she would sometimes reply, "Oh, yes, but I think we did it more for the sound of the thing than anything else."

Her companion would shake her head, puzzled.

"Ménage à trois. It sounds so nice, so civilized and sophisticated. Quite different from 'bigamy' or 'screwing two women'." And then, if she really wanted to be shocking, she would add, "Although, after a while, it sounded more like 'ménage à twat' to me." And then, it really was time to change the subject.

She bought a handbook of French-Canadian words and phrases at Classics the afternoon before, and she has brought it with her to show him. Walking along St. Catherine's Street, she sees in the window of a restaurant: PAIN DORÉ. "Golden pain" is the first thing that comes to her; then, "golden bread." She stops to look it up. "Canada: *Pain doré*. France: *Pain perdu*. French Toast." Of course. But, in her present state of mind, she likes her first interpretation better—"golden pain." The real thing. Or what about "pain perdu"? That was pretty good too. Pain forever lost.

They both liked fooling around with words. They had gone on a trip to Rome together, just the two of them, in the early days of their relationship. They sat in the Forum, eating bread and sausage, and reading to each other out of the phrase book.

"I have no appetite. I get indigestion."

"Oh oon dee-stoor-boh dee stoh'-mah-koh."

"'Oh lah feb'ray.' I have fever."

"Mee sahng'gwee-nah eel nah'soh."

She flipped the pages.

"Guess this one? 'Kwell oo-oh'moh me say'gway dahp-pehr-toot'-toh."

They were both laughing so hard that they could barely speak.

"I like the dahp-pehr-toot'-toh," he said. "Something like, 'where do I find a trumpet player'?"

"No. It means 'everywhere.' 'That man is following me every-where'."

"Maybe we'd better stick to *veni, vidi, vici*."

Later that day, she discovered that a *letto matrimoniale* was a 'double bed.' But she didn't show him that one, as he was still officially matrimonio to someone else.

Once, after he had gone back to his wife, but they were all still in Montreal, they had been in a bar on Mountain Street, where a girl whom he and his wife had known from years past came up to them and said hello. She asked what they had been doing. No mention was made of the long break-up, or of his time with her, or of their reconciliation—of course not. She sat there feeling as if she had been erased, as easily as one erases a name from a blackboard. Rubbed out, the way sometimes the boys in her grade three class had been made to sand down their names and initials, until they disappeared. It was as though her time with him hadn't meant anything, as though, in their official history, she was not going to be mentioned, not even as a footnote. They would change the dates and stretch things, and pretty soon, there would be no gaps—all their time past would be accounted for. She did not blame them—in their place, she would probably have done the same—but she hated them for doing it. They did this thing in front of her, knowing that she would not publicly contradict them. She was not the sort to make scenes in public places.

("He's not even *nice*," my daughter says to me, puzzled. "He's mean to us and he's mean to the little kids. There are a lot of boys who are nicer than he is."

"Niceness doesn't seem to have much to do with it," I say.)

"Bonjour là," she says, "I'm sorry that I'm late." He looks at his watch. "Actually, you're two minutes early." They do not kiss, but as he stands up, they lean a little towards each other and then straighten up. He gives her a big smile (reels her in, reels her in); he is genuinely pleased to see her.

"Before I forget, I have an invitation for you. We would like you to come to dinner tomorrow night, if you're free." We. We would like. "I can't," she says. "There is an official banquet. But I'm free in the afternoon—or can arrange to be. There are a lot of papers being given. Everyone will think that I'm somewhere else. Maybe Sheila would like to go to the Hundertwasser exhibition and out to tea at that Hungarian tearoom. I'll call her tonight, shall I?" They have begun walking; she has forgotten how long his legs are, how fast he walks. In the French-Canadian handbook, she has marked a page to show him. "Look," she will say over lunch, "In France, you are 'un homme grand et efflanqué.' Over here, you are 'un grand slaque.' I like that. My mother would have called you 'a long drink of water'."

They will have ordered a carafe of white wine.

"Are you still taking French lessons?" he asks.

"Oh yes, at the Alliance Française. But there is no chance to speak it. And you?"

"Both of us. We'll be ready when the revolution comes."

(Canada: *casser*. France: *rompre*, to break up). They make polite conversation and wait for the food to come.

The winter before, living around the corner from them in an old apartment building, seeing them two or three times a week, she met a woman at a bus stop whose face had frozen two weeks before. They had to take her to Emergency. "It's when your face feels really warm that you're in trouble," she said through her thick woollen scarf. "That's the frostbite beginning. You'd better wrap up more."

We used to come in from sledding, in my New York state childhood, and our mother would stick our feet in pans of lukewarm water. There was so much to put on and take off then; leggings (another obsolete word), and mittens, which hung on elastics threaded through your coatsleeves, and black galoshes, with nasty black metal fasteners which became full of packed snow and hurt your fingers to unfasten. Out here, on the British Columbia coast, winter is easier and gentler. We have had one week of snow this year—in January—and *that* was unusual. School was dismissed early on the second snowy day, for fear that the bus wouldn't make the hills. My daughter and I put on long underwear, underneath our jeans, and took pieces of heavy plastic sheeting off the woodpile and slid down all the steep driveways that belong to the weekend and summer people. Then, we came home, soaked and laughing, and had cocoa. It

164

had started to snow again, and the world outside our cottage looked as though it were full of chicken feathers. I told my daughter about a wonderful sled that my sister and I owned when we were children. An old sled, fixed up by our grandfather, repainted by him, a nice fire-engine red. It was called a "Flexible Flyer" and it could really steer. I told her how some steep streets in our town would be blocked off by the police when the heavy snows came, and then, the children would be allowed to go sledding at night. I told her about the big boys, who would jump on back, just as we got going, and zig-zag us dangerously down the hill, trying to steer us into garbage cans that had been put out at the curb, until Somebody's Mother, hearing all the screams and commotion, would come to her front door, apron still on from doing the dinner dishes, and tell them to leave the little kids alone, that they ought to be ashamed of themselves, big boys like that. I tell her about snowballs with lumps of coal in them, but also about maple syrup heated and poured on fresh snow; about skating at Recreation Park to: "I'm Looking Over a Four Leaf Clover That I Overlooked Before." She likes to hear stories about my youth. I watch her as she listens and drinks her cocoa, the cat asleep on her lap. She is twelve years old and teetering on the edge. Never again will she be as free as she is now.

After the woman at the bus stop on Côte Saint-Luc told her about her face freezing and thawing again, she thought of how she seemed to have put her heart in some freezing solution, some freezer drawer, and she trembled at the thought of how much it was going to hurt if she ever let it thaw out again. "The pain was terrible," the woman said, "and then, it itched so. And then, it peeled. I'd bundle up more, if I were you." On particularly snowy, slippery days, cars sped through red lights, their drivers unable to brake, horns honking wildly. The buses were full of the smell of wet wool and fur.

When I went away to college for the first time, my mother gave me her, by now, standard lecture on promiscuity, but, this time, she added a codicil on drinking. If I had to accept a drink at a dance or a party, if I really felt I *had* to, I was to take a token sip or two, and then pour the rest into a nearby potted palm.

"A potted palm! A potted palm!" How I laughed at her! I shrieked with contemptuous laughter. My mother had me quite late and I realized that she was still back in the early twenties sometime, repeating something that *her* mother must have said to her. But it was all right. I went to a nice college and the boys that I was introduced to on weekends or on blind dates were nice boys. They went elsewhere for their sex.

In Rome, they had walked down stone steps to the river, and she had taken his picture by the Tiber. There were graffiti everywhere and the smell of pee.

"Let Rome in Tiber melt," she said.

"What's that?"

"Oh, just the words of another great lover, Marc Antony."

(Angelo loved Sophia. Roman girls were _____. Well, she didn't know what the word meant, but she could guess.)

The ides of February are come. Aye, Madam, but not yet gone. I could take the butter out of the cupboard and put it nearer the stove. It is very cold today and we have no central heating. If the butter stays over there in the cupboard, it won't mix well. I could even make the cupcakes in a little while, and leave the girls to ice and decorate them. I could go out and chop wood. All this sitting down isn't good for me; I need some exercise. I could write a letter to my old mother, or to one of my other daughters. I could get the garbage ready to take down to the Solid Waste Disposal Area (the Dump). I could wash the kitchen floor. It really isn't wise to begin something as important as this story on the ides of the month. I will turn the candy hearts over, shuffle them like cards, draw one; see if I can find an answer. I select a yellow one, chosen at random, and turn it up. "DON'T BE A DRIP," it says.

When they have finished their lunch, he will suggest that they walk around for a while, down towards Old Montreal, and have a drink at the Hotel Nelson. She has never been inside there, and readily agrees. The sidewalk cafés are all shut up and they are the only people, except for the barmaid, in the bar of the hotel. They sit by the dusty windows and order a beer. He tells her that it was from this hotel that the news about Pierre Laporte was announced. But she doesn't want to talk about past history of any kind. A silence falls upon them. She looks at his long, fine hands on the table.

"You're looking good," he says. "That's a real nice skirt."

"Oh, I got it at a sale," she lies. In fact, once she knew that she was coming to this conference, she searched and searched for just the right outfit to meet him in, something stylish yet demure. When they lived together, he was always telling her to button up her blouse. So she knew just what to look for. She wanted to look good; she wanted to proclaim by the way that she was dressed, "Well, *I'm* all right!"

"I have to be home by three-thirty," he says, glancing at his watch. "Did Sheila tell you we have a puppy?"

"She may have mentioned it, I don't remember."

"Well, we do. I promised that I wouldn't stay away from the little fella too long. He's only six weeks old."

"What happens when the strike ends?"

"Oh, it won't end for a while. And he'll be older then. And Sheila's only substituting, you know. She doesn't work every day."

She knows that she is supposed to ask what kind of puppy it is, what's its name, all the appropriate things. After all, he has enquired about her children. But instead, she makes patterns with the damp rings on the table.

"Tell me that you miss me?" she says. There is no answer and she does not look up.

Finally, he says, "Why do you want to torture me?"

She pulls out the French-Canadian handbook and they start going through it. Some of the swear words, "Les Sacres," have not been translated, and he, who was born here, tells her, more or less, what they mean in English.

"It's interesting how the Québécois, perhaps all Catholics?, use church words as sexual metaphors. We don't have any equivalent to that in English."

"Well, they just combine the two most taboo things. The church doesn't have the same power in the Protestant world."

They look at the difference between "parking" in Canada and France.

"'Se peloter dans une voiture et dans un endroit isolé,' as

opposed to 'faire du parking'."

"Simplification," he says. "Actually, can you imagine some French guy asking a girl if she wants to 'te peloter dans ma voiture et dans un endroit isolé?' I can't believe that he would really say that. He probably just goes up and grabs her ass."

They stand on the corner of Notre Dame and Place Jacques Cartier and wait for the light to change. Just as they step off the curb, the light turns red and he pulls her back. "Arrêtez," says the signal. Suddenly, she runs right into the middle of the traffic (there really isn't much traffic); she, who is always so cautious about crossing streets; she, who was told last year that she could never become "une vraie Montréalaise" until she learned to ignore the lights. Some horns blare, but she makes it safely to the other side.

"Tell me that you miss me!" she calls to him. "Just say it. Just admit it." He stands on the other side of the street, a tall, handsome, loose-limbed man, "un grand slaque, un homme grand et efflanqué," her ex-lover, her love, grinning, shaking his head.

"Tell me that you miss me or I'll walk away forever!" Again, he shakes his head and smiles, so she turns her back on him and begins to walk in the direction of the Métro.

"I miss you, you bitch! Tabarnac! I miss you!" She stops.

Then, remembering how Sally Bowles/Liza Minelli said goodbye to her Christopher Isherwood/Michael York boyfriend in *Cabaret,* she reaches her right hand over her left shoulder and, wishing that she had Minelli's green fingernails, she waves goodbye.

And she doesn't look back. In my story, that is. She doesn't look back in my story.

## TALONBOOKS—FICTION IN PRINT 1981

*Songs My Mother Taught Me*—Audrey Thomas
*Blown Figures*—Audrey Thomas
*Hungry Hills*—George Ryga
*Theme for Diverse Instruments*—Jane Rule
*Mrs. Blood*—Audrey Thomas
*Night Desk*—George Ryga
*Ballad of a Stonepicker*—George Ryga
*Dürer's Angel*—Marie-Claire Blais
*A Short Sad Book*—George Bowering
*Desert of the Heart*—Jane Rule
*The School-Marm Tree*—Howard O'Hagan
*The Woman Who Got on at Jasper Station
 & Other Stories*—Howard O'Hagan
*Wilderness Men*—Howard O'Hagan
*Latakia*—Audrey Thomas
*The Con Man*—Ken Mitchell
*Prisoner of Desire*—britt hagarty
*The Fat Woman Next Door Is Pregnant*—Michel Tremblay
*Real Mothers*—Audrey Thomas
*Sad Paradise*—britt hagarty